IMANI'S DIARY

DO NOT TOUCH OR
READ MY F****N STUFF

CHANTEL HALL-REID

Imani's Diary authored by Chantel Hall-Reid
©Chantel Hall-Reid 2020
Cover Design Charlene Hemans of Marcia M Publshing House
Editing – Aisha Otiti of Marcia M Publishing House
Assisted by Shelly Allmark of Marcia M Publshing House

Published by Marcia M Spence of MARCIA M PUBLISHING HOUSE LTD in West Bromwich B71
In the United Kingdom

MARCIA M
PUBLISHING HOUSE

www.marciampublishing.com

This is a work of fiction. Names, characters, places, and incidents are either the product of the authors imagination, or, if real, used fictitiously. All statements, activities, descriptions, information, and material of any kind contained herein are included for entertainment purposes only and should not be relied on for accuracy or replicated as they may result in injury.

Any opinions, statements, views are those of the author who has created this work of FICTION and not those of the Marcia M Publishing House Ltd or any subcontracted editors, proofreaders or designers.

DEDICATION

This book is dedicated to all those who enjoy a good read and just want to escape the daily routine of life and be transported back to a period in time where life was fun, carefree and at times a little crazy!

It's also dedicated to the lost souls, to those who didn't really feel accepted, wanted or a sense of belonging and never really understood why. It's to the females that may have felt violated by friends, family and boys who thought they were men. It's to the females that were trying to discover themselves and had to fathom things out alone.

To the females that longed to feel love and sought it from literally anybody that passed their way. To the females who are now on a journey of self-worth and self-love.

This book is also dedicated to all those who have a dream of writing, this is proof that you can achieve anything you want as long as you believe in yourself and put your mind to it. Believe in your vision, set an intention, and turn it into a goal, oh and then plan!!! (I love a plan!) Set actionable steps. You've got this!! Enjoy!!

OH, and finally, one last dedication. To all those people that have EVER read someone's diary, this is for you. This time you can read it with permission!

IMANI'S DIARY

DO NOT READ

So, you've decided to read MY diary.
Do you know the level of disrespect that this is?

The sheer violation!

But that's not gonna stop you, is it?

I mean, you've managed to get this far haven't you.

Okay, well seen as you're so dyammm nosey, I'm gonna give you something to read.
You've been warned!

1996

27th December 1996

I've decided to start a diary. I've been thinking about it for a while. The other day Mrs Kumar accidently left the stock cupboard open; we all ran in and teefed pure stationery. I jacked this notebook knowing I was gonna start a diary soon.

~~Dear Diary.~~ Nah, dear diary sounds too kiddy.

Toady had been planned for a while still. A few days ago, Trayvon asked me to wrap a present for his mom 'cause his wrapping skills are rubbish. When he came to pick up the present, he said that my wrapping skills were wifey skills. That's the day we made our plans to link up 'officially'. We both planned what was gonna happen. I knew I wanted to link him before the year was done, plus I'm 14 in January and everyone else 'has done it'.

I've liked him for YEARS. He's quite tall, don't ask me 'bout exact measurements 'cause maths aint my strong point. I just know he's taller than me and I like that. His skin is smooth, you can tell he looks after himself, no rough looking boy. He always walks around with Vaseline for his lips, when he licks them he reminds me of LL Cool J. He's got short black hair that he keeps real low and he dresses sharp, designers and all a dat. Even when he aint wearing designers, he looks sharp. Sometimes he busses grey contact lenses, yo he looks sexy with them in.

Mom went to do some sound check and vocal rehearsals today, so I met Trayvon in the bus station for 5pm. Our bus never came until 5.20pm it felt like we were waiting for ages. Yo the 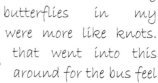 butterflies in my stomach, well they were more like knots. The exact planning that went into this made waiting around for the bus feel even longer, even if it was only an extra 20 minutes! We went to his house through the back door. There was this silly white cat on the garden fence, I said "move the silly cat man," he said I mustn't diss the cat 'cause the cat hasn't done anything to me. His dad's girlfriend was there, she offered us a dairy milk chocolate, but I didn't want any. I was probably just too shook to be honest. Trayvon said something sarcastic like "she's gonna get some chocolate in a bit." She didn't have a clue what he was on about. Him and his code words and phrases! DICKHEAD, making it bait.

We went into his room; it was quite small, it was painted in baby blue with a border going around the top and his carpet looked rubbed out boy. There were a few posters on the walls; Aaliyah, TOTAL, Adina Howard and SWV I think, well he's gonna get a shock 'cause my figure don't look like none of theirs!

I asked him if he'd been buying Smash hits magazines on the sly to have that many posters. He just laughed.

He had a small single bed with Simpson bedsheets, ha, ha. When he's on road he acts like a big man and he's got Simpson bed sheets you know!! I said sarcastically, "what's with the Simpson bedsheets!" He acted like he didn't hear me.

2

He was playing Adina Howard, 'freak in the morning and a freak in the evening.' I love that song. I don't know whether the tune was coincidence, a hidden message or if I was being para, but this was my first time, so no freaky business was gonna be runnin'. I was sat there on his bed, waiting for him to tell me what to do, I guess! Then he said something like "aren't you gonna take your clothes off?" To be fair he was probably wondering why I was just sat on the bed like some dyam arse.

I took off my leggings but I left my top on. Don't ask me why. What were the rules? I wonder if I looked stupid with it on...hmm! Too late now, plus he never asked me to take it off, so I guess it was ok. He turned the lights off and I just lay on the bed, singing the lyrics to Adina Howard in my head. We started lipsing. Then he put my legs over his shoulders, then we started; one thing led to another.

Afterwards we lay on the bed and I was telling him I can't believe I've liked him since Aug 95. He asked what I liked about him, I said I didn't know and that I just thought he was kriss How dumb did that sound? No Imani, you could've said something wayyy better than that. When we were lying down and I had my arm around him, I felt sweet.

I went downstairs and I filled Monique in on what had happened. She was telling me that while she was waiting for me, Caleb, Trayvon's best friend was begging her for a shine. I could only imagine how trampy he was going on. We aint no shiners.

3

Monique's my ride or die best friend. We both have matching gold necklaces that we got from Argos, hers says 'best' and mine says 'friend's'. We are similar in some ways but quite different in others. She lives with her mom in a massive house whereas I live with my mom and two sisters in a smaller house. Her mom's a big-time women's right community worker and my mom's a singer. Monique's bedroom is kitted out whereas I share mine with Janay. Monique's got bare stuff. She aint got any brothers or sisters that's probably why Marcia spoils her.

I've got two sisters: Janay (Older) and Chana (younger). I'm the middle kid. Chana is into her Tamagotchi, pure foolishness. She's created this little pet that she's gotta keep alive by looking after it, she's addicted to it.

Janay's older than me, she's got a part time job at the Fun Factory. It's this place for kids parties I think she serves food in there. Janay uses most of her money to go out partying with her friends. Her best friend is Alisha. She's got short hair like the main singer in TOTAL. They're all into House n Garage music. I like it, but not as much as Janay.

Anyway, Caleb A.K.A Devious (we call him Devious 'cause he's such a sneaky piece of shit) was downstairs, he said, "*Imani walk across the room.*" It was probably to see if I was walking funny after losing my virginity. Caleb's such a DICKHEAD. I think I was walking alright to be fair. But later on, my legs were paining me some ways. I think

Trayvon's kriss. I hate the fact that he knows how much I like him. Imani what were you thinking?

<u>Rule NO:1 NEVER EVER TELL THEM HOW MUCH YOU LIKE THEM</u>.

Straight fail for me. He hasn't even phoned me to see if I've got home OK though. Wha' the hell. Some joke ting.

Imani's Diary

1997

It's been 6 months since the kidnap ting at Chana's school. They were having some kind of teddy bear picnic to celebrate the end of the school term and one mad woman jumped over the fence and tried to grab one of the kids. Mom said that her and the other parents were trying to distract the woman, but she just started grabbing random kids. Mad ting. I'm so glad that Chana was ok though. I should ask her how she is, no-ones really talked to her about it. I know I haven't.

19th Jan 1997

Today's my birthday, 14 Jheeze. The day was ok I suppose, mom gave me some money and my dad came down and dropped off a card with fifty quid in there. Couple family members came round but I weren't in the mood to be honest. I came on my period today and my stomachs been killing me. Everyone said I looked miserable but I aint gonna exactly say it's 'cause I'm on my reds am I.

My Uncle Vincent came down and bought me a cake. I don't even like cake! He's got no clue I swear. He either forgets my birthday altogether and then, on the rare occasions that he does remember he buys me a fukin walnut and mint chocolate cake . They're the worst flavour combo's ever, why wouldn't you just buy vanilla or chocolate? Walnut you

know. Ewwww. He can take that shit back with him. I aint eating that. He lives about 2 hours from us, so we only see him once or twice a year, thank God. He hardly calls us and he just lives a separate life. Can't really call him an uncle, he's just an uncle by title.

He doesn't look anything like mom and his features are way different. He's got wavey hair whereas moms got dreadlocks. He acts posh, whereas moms just down to earth. He thinks 'cause he lives outta town that he's made it, and he kinda looks down on us. Dickhead. I aint interested in him to be fair.

I was so glad when everyone went, I phoned Monique for a bit and chilled. She said she'd bought me some tarot cards for my birthday. She knows how much I'm into all that stuff, I'll get them off her the next time I see her.
Anyway, I'm getting off, stomachs killing me, I can't wait for this period to be over and done with.

24th Jan 1997
Today I went to youth club, it was OK. Saw some of the Hit Squad Crew. There's about 15 of them and they all buss different coats; Raiders, Mighty Ducks, Michigan, Chicago Bulls, Charlotte Hornets, they walk round like they're bad. We all love the Hit Squad Crew though and they know how much the girls love them too. They've all got bare gyal, but they try to keep their girls 'undercover'.

25th Jan 1997
Went to town today with Monique. I gave this nice boy Floyd my phone number. He said he was 17 and that he goes to college. He had golden skin like he'd just come off a holiday or something and his features were

sharp. He looked like he takes care of himself, skin looked smooth no bumps or nuen. His hair had a slight wave in it, and he looked tick. I know he's three years older than me, so what? He was saying that he's studying Music Production and wants to be a DJ when he's older. He was saying that he plays at carnivals to get his practice in. He was with .his friend Devante; I was quite surprised when Floyd started talking to me, 'cause I thought he would have gone for Monique. Devante was ok looking too, but a bit darker.

I never got anything from town, we just grabbed a burger from McDonalds. We saw Trayvon, but he just bopped straight past me. I asked Monique to find out why he was blanking me. When she came back she said he wasn't talking to me 'cause I dissed his silly white cat that he loves. My manz really beks over the cat you know, KISS MY TEETH. He weren't bothered 'bout no cat when I was in his bed couple weeks ago though was he, that's fukin pissed me off.

26th Jan 1997
Floyd called me today, said he'd call at 7, but didn't call till 8.15pm. Not tha lique. He was saying that he's into sports and loves playing football. He said that he drinks loads of water too 'cause he likes to keep fit. I was like, ok Floyd that's what we like to hear. We were on the phone for quite a while still.

Went to dad's house today, it's massive. The joke is it's just the two of them there; him and his wife Nina. At the front of

9

the house, they've got a drive with bare space for pure cars and a garage. The front garden is sharp it's got lots of plants and stuff, I know Nina sorted that 'cause my dad aint no gardener! Gardening is an old peoples ting.

When you walk inside the house theres a massive hall with a crystal chandelier dangling from the ceiling. Further down the hall theres a massive living room, it's got a stush marble fireplace with a charcoal fire. They've even got a separate dining room with a patio door to the back garden. I doubt they even eat in there to be honest. Probably just for show! Then they've got a breakfast kitchen with matching cupboards you know, mad ting. Plus, it's got a built-in separate area for the washing machine and tumble dryer. Dad says it's Nina's place 'fe iron and sart out de mess;' Nina calls it a 'utility room'. No-one can chat to my dad when it comes to his yard, its dark. Bare people would wanna live in that area it's proper stush up there still.

Anyway, back to his wife Nina. She was at the house when I went there. I'm not even sure how I feel about her to be honest. Dads only been married for a few months. At their wedding she wore this tunic style dress, big, big wedding day and it looked like a work dress, tight and boring, a bit like her really! But true it was Calvin Klein, she had to buss it. I think Calvin Klein's range is dry, come in like the fabric is rigid and can't stretch, it suits Nina 'cause their design pieces are "stiff."

I remember the man in the church at their wedding saying, "Do you Nina Harrington-Bechtel take Donald Evans to be your lawful wedded husband?" Harrington-Bechtel?? Who the fuk has a double barrel surname? That's how you know she's posh and from Cambridge. What a come down

'Evans' must be from her heighty tighty maiden name. I hate that me and her have got the same surname now, people will think she's my mom, fukin hell man.

She looks older than my dad, I'm not sure on the exact age, but she looks old and miserable. All I know is that she's a health freak and works as a Mortgage Advisor. She has her hair scraped back tight in a ponytail, so her cheekbones and features stick out even more. She keeps her hair neat and tidy, like an air hostess, not one strand outta place. Her make up is sharp and she usually wears a light pink lipstick with a darker lip liner. She's got a beauty spot underneath her eyes; she mus' think she's the singer Neneh Cherry. Ha.

27th Jan 1997
Floyd phoned me today; he was giving me joke. He was asking if I'm with anyone, as in, am I seeing anyone. Well, Trayvon aint talking to me, (white cat) so technically the answers no isn't it? Plus, we aint even with each other like that anyway. So, I said yeah I'm single.

Monique and Kim came to mine, we were chilling watching MTVBase and ketchin some joke. Kim was singing Diana King 'Shy Guy' in patios it was so funny. Us lot were creasing! Kim's my bredrin still, we have our ups and downs, but she's ok most of the time. She always wears butterfly clips in her hair and has this bright purple puffer jacket that she wears everywhere! Because she hangs around with us; nuff gyal don't like her, they reckon she thinks she's black. Fools. Kim was asking Janay to put her hair in 'Chinney bumps'. Janay did Kim's hair then went to her friend Alisha's house.

11

29th Jan 1997

Floyd phoned at midnight, he was meant to call me at 6.30pm, but said 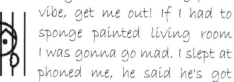 he went ice skating and forgot. He doesn't know time at all. It's a good job mom weren't at home 'cause 12pm's a piss take, she was out with 'The Conscious Sisters Group'. She's a backing singer. Kim slept at mine today, she was telling me how her little sister's been doing her head in and how her stepdad always takes her side. I was like that's some madness. Kim's mom's hardly home; she works as a nurse so Kim's just left with her stepdad and her little sis, the shit stirrer. She was telling me that her stepdad can't cook, and he always buys microchips and its pissin' her off. She asked if Janay can show her how to cook stir fry pork. Yo, I had to tell her we don't eat trenton round here, yuh mad. My dad's from yard and moms a Rasta, no star; pork's banned from this house. I told Kim not to even mention the word pork in our house, pigs are the narstiest animal around, they eat anytin'.

I should ask Kim to ask her mom about how I can get into nursing, I've been thinking about doing it for a while. But bwoy if I had kids, they'd never see me 'cause the hours that Kim's mom works are madness. If you have kids you should find a job that means you can still be there with them.

29th Jan 1997

I needed to get out the house today. Same old boring faces, same old boring vibe, get me out! If I had to look at the same sponge painted living room walls any longer I was gonna go mad. I slept at Kim's. Floyd phoned me, he said he's got something he needs to ask me tomorrow so to make sure I'm back home by 3pm so I can answer the phone. I wonder what he wants to ask me.

30th Jan 1997

Had strawberry Pop Tarts at Kim's this morning. She was saying they tasted better in the microwave, what kinda' nonsense was she on about. Everyone knows Pop Tarts DON'T GO IN THE MICROWAVE. Left Kim's around 2pm and hurried back to mine to wait for Floyds call. I sat there looking at the phone for ages, our house phone is see through and lights up when someone calls. Floyd didn't phone me AT ALL today. I could've chilled with Kim longer.

31st Jan 1997

Youth club was so dry. Moms gone to America today for

four weeks, she's got a big tour over there with The Conscious Sisters, so Janay is looking after me and Chana. Moms friend Sonia lives around the corner and we've got Gaynor next door, so we are cool.

Sonia and Gaynor are mom's best friends, Sonia has got the same birthday as mom, she's got short brown hair and she wears it in a bob and she's mixed race. She's got thin lips and good skin, she uses that Oil of Ulay, she gets it from Avon, I've seen it in her bathroom. She always looks nice when I see her. She works at Kwik Save and gets mom and Gaynor bare discounts. It's a bit shameful though 'cause all the stuff from Kwik Save comes in this no frills packaging, its black and white and says 'No Frills' in big letters, it looks kinda cheap.

Gaynor's nice, she lives next door to us but she's a bit of a random. She's an older white lady, she wears random clothes that don't match, and she's got a Jamaican flag in her living room. She's funny man, I swear. She's proper quirky and down to earth. She's originally from Yorkshire but moved down here for a change of scenery.

Can't believe moms going for four weeks it's a long time man. Wish we could go with her; I'd love to go to America.

2nd Feb 1997

Floyd phoned, he asked me if I wanted to start going out with him. JHEZE, Sooooooooo I'm checkin' him (at last) my manz tick. Oh, and he told me to tell Monique that she can check his friend Devante if she wants! Janay was moaning today saying moms been gone one day and the house was like a pig sty, calm down Janay, your exaggerating. Fukin hell.

3rd Feb 1997

Floyd and Devante wanted to come down today, but I told them to come on Wednesday instead. I went Central Station Youth Club with Monique; no-one was up there. When I got back, I phoned Floyd. I put about 90p in the phone box, we only got halfway through the convo then my money ran out. I forgot to bring a pound for the phone box scam. I don't even know if we are checkin' properly. I'll ask him the next time he calls. Sometimes it seems like I'm his girl then other times I feel like I'm just his friend.

Kim's man is getting lock up (again). I'm sure it's for 7 years this time. Some joke ting. I swear he's about 25 years old, if Kath ever found out about the age difference, she would be phoning leng I'm telling yah. I've told Kim that he's wayyy too old, but she always says that she can't get out of it. She was telling me how he locked her in his flat before I can't remember the ins and outs, but my man is psycho. He's got a tattoo on his face and one above his eyebrow too, he looks like a mad man. We heard his ex gyal pressed charges on him for GBH and now he's finally being sentenced. I remember at the time him telling Kim that it was all bullshit, well look now, lock him up yes. Fukin liar.

DICKHEAD
I'm glad he's locked up, maybe Kim can link someone decent now.

5th Feb 1997
Went to Central Station Youth Club with Monique, it was ok, loads of people were up there. Everyone knows that Kim's man is lock up and got 7 years, everyone's been talking about it. Spoke to Kim's mom about nursing today, she said it was draining and that I shouldn't bother. It can't be that bad, why's she still there?

6th Feb 1997
I heard that Lachelle's been chattin' me, but she can go and piss off. She's a BITCH, HOE, TRAMP, SKETTEL. She really does my head in you know; I swear. One minute we're fine then the next minute she talks 'bout me or does something mad behind my back.

Janay's made dinner: chicken stir fry, it tasted dark, Janay can proper cook. I phoned Kim today, she told me she had Crispy beef Pancakes for dinner with packet Smash, bwoy sah.

15

7th Feb 1997

I went to Midpoint Youth Club today it was pure joke, plus it made a change from going to Central Station Youth Club. Before I went though, I did some cooking with Gaynor, she's quite old and needs help around the house, she pays me to do odd jobs for her. I made her cheese and potato pie and beans; she was cool with that. I like Gaynor though, she's proper down to earth and when I'm there she takes the time to listen to me. She always tells me stories about what life was like when she was a headteacher, she's retired now. I feel sorry for Gaynor sometimes 'cause all her family live in Yorkshire, she moved down here after her husband died years ago and wanted a change of scenery (you don't choose the Midlands though do yah). Her daughter Eileen still lives in Yorkshire, but Gaynor doesn't talk to her. Gaynor don't play you know, a few years ago Gaynor had a cancer scare so Eileen came down to look after her, Gaynor was telling me how she caught Eileen teefin' money out of her purse. The next day when she asked Eileen, she denied it. From that day to this Gaynor aint spoken to her. It's bad though because Eileen's got a kid now, Charlie, I think his name is and Gaynor has never seen him. I know she'd like to meet him one day, after all it is her grandson.

Kim's sleeping at mine tonight; she's stressed about the idiot being locked up and everyone knowing. I told her she's better off without him anyway; there's no way he can love her when he treats her like a joey, making her do EVERYTHING for him, like some rarse skivvy.

12th Feb 1997

Spoke to Floyd, put in arl a £3. The phone box at the bottom of Deakon Street is shit. The scam wasn't working so I'm bruk now. Janay said I couldn't go out today and that I needed to look after Chana, I don't mind though to be fair. Chana aint no trouble at all, she plays with her Tamagotchi and begs me to play Mouse Trap with her. That board game is so dry.

14th Feb 1997

I went to a Valentines party in Beacon Village with Monique, it was ok. I wore some red lace leggings with a denim skirt and a red top.

I had a red bandana around my head with a piece gelled down and the rest in a ponytail, yooooo I looked dark. I had some 's' curls gelled down too, yo that Nyxon gel got my 's' curls looking sharp. We stayed at the party till about 3am.

15th Feb 1997

Janay said I could go town, but I better not take the piss up there. Saw all of the Hit Squad Crew in town today. Jheeze them man are tick. I saw Imogen on the way to town, she's ok still. She's not someone I'd class as a proper bredrin, but she lives close, so more time we just say whar gwarn to each other. Sometimes she comes to mine and sometimes I go to hers. She dresses like those American geeks; you know with the dungarees and the striped t-shirts underneath. Every time I see her, she's got a rucksack on (nothin' aint in there, it's just part of the look) she wears her hair in two ponytails and even wears braces. Her teeth are fine.

17th Feb 1997
Me and Monique were meant to meet Floyd and Devante, but we never ended up seeing them. We arranged to meet outside the McDonalds, we waited there for at least 40 minutes like idiots. When we were walking back to get the train, these other boys started to chat to us. I couldn't even be bothered to chat to them, then they started to shout out how we think we're too nice and how we aint got no manners. We hot stepped to the train. We weren't looking to get into anything with those mad manz.

18th Feb 1997
Went town, saw couple people up there. Janay told me to make sure I didn't spend too long in town.

19th Feb 1997
Nuff outta town man were in bus station today, looking tick. Jheeze.

20th Feb 1997
Went to bus depot about 10.30pm, everyone was there, stayed there for a bit and caught some joke. Janay cooked dinner for me and Chana, it was really nice. Them lot had a swiss roll for pudding. I hate sponge, worse still it's with strawberry jam filling, disgusting.

21st Feb 1997
Midpoint Youth Club was dark, everyone was there. Dejuan was there begging me to go out with him. He's good looking, to be fair he's been asking Monique to ask me out for him for ages, and since Floyds stood me up, I guess I'm single. I said yeah in the end, so I'm checkin' Dejuan now.

22nd Feb 1997

Went to a party today with Monique and Kim. Kim got Janay to do her hair, she had half gelled down and the rest in a big 'Chinney bump,' it looked ok still. We weren't sure if it would hold true her hair texture aint like ours, but it looked ok. Towards the end of the night nuff fights broke out. Leng came and everyone got off. No one was looking to get lock up!

23rd Feb 1997

Phoned Dejuan today, he wasn't saying much, he seemed a bit dry, he weren't talking anything constructive.

Janay was telling me that the kids at her workplace were doing her head in, she was saying that the kids kept chucking all the balls out of the ball pit, so she had to keep going round and putting them back in!! I bet that was doing her head in 'cause she's a clean freak, she hates mess.

24th Feb 1997

Went to town today, I bought a new Naff Naff jacket, it looks dark. Can't wait to buss that at school tomorrow. Mines the proper ting, no fake version like them gyal are wearing that they got from the market!

26th Feb 1997

Everyone was at Midpoint, saw Dejuan, he was being a bit quiet again today, I asked him what was up, but he said he was fine. Nuff people were askin' 'bout my jacket today, saying it looked dark, yo don't watch me!

27th Feb 1997
Banged Dejuan after school today. Was a quick ting.

28th Feb 1997
Moms back from touring America. When I got home from school I saw her suitcase in the hallway, four weeks she's been gone for, I was so happy she was home. She even said we could have a Chinese for dinner; while we were eating she said she was only back for 4-5 days 'cause she's got another tour. Joke ting.

Mom used to work as a Manager at Beatties before she got into singing.

One day she came back from work and told us that she wasn't going back. She never said why. Me and Janay think it's something to do with her having dreadlocks or wearing a Rasta cap. We heard her on the phone to Sonia saying something like "What else did they expect me to wear to keep the locks out of my face and that the colours (red, yellow green and black) weren't appropriate." From that day on she's been singing with The Conscious Sisters.

1st March 1997
Today's Nyah's Birthday
We all went to hers after school. She lives with her aunty. She cooked pure food for us and we all chilled round there. Nyah can nyam you know, she had like three plates. Their house is full of African pictures and wooden statues, looks like some kinda African jungle. I remember one time at school in PSHE, we were learning about the effects of alcohol, two twos Nyah ran out the class, everyone was like what's goin on? The next

day Nyah told me that the reason she ran out the class was 'cause it reminded her about her mom's drinking problems and that's partly why she lives with her aunt. She was telling me that her mom used to work as a prostitute and there was just pure man in and out the house when she was younger. Madness, I swear everyone's family is fuked.

2nd March 1997
Got my hair done in some curly plaits, they look dark. Went to Nyah's today she was saying that one of her uncles has died and that she's gotta go to America for the funeral. Then I heard her aunt on the phone to someone, she said *"Ek dink ons het vlugte nodig."* I asked Nyah what she was saying, Nyah told me that she's looking for flights to **Africa**. I said, "Africa? I thought you said your uncle lived in America?" Nyah begged me not to tell anyone her family were really from Africa. I burst out laughing, yoooooooo I've got one over on her now. If anyone finds out she's from AFRICA, she will get dissed big time.

4th March 1997
Everyone knows I'm checkin Dejuan now, people are soooooooo chat.

5th March 1997
Went Midpoint, Dejuan was there he looked tick. We were sitting and chattin' on the wall for ages. He had his arm around me all night.

Moms gone to Denmark; I think she's back on the 22nd. She's got back to back shows all month.

6th March 1997
Nothing really happened at all today. Janay was moaning about Chana spilling some Nesquik chocolate on the kitchen sides, I had to remind her it was an accident, calm down Janay. It can be wiped up.

7th March 1997
Can't even remember what happened today.

8th March 1997
Lost my pager last week Saturday, I'm so beks. Went Rising Star Blues . It was in someone's yard and we were all just squash up inside the main room dancing, think we paid about £1 to get in, we caught pure joke. Me and Monique slept at Kim's. We got back to Kim's at 7.30am. Her stepdad was moaning about the time. Kath was on a late shift so that was ok. The Blues was dark, everyone was there including Dejuan. We were dancing most of the night together. Couple arguments bruked out 'cause one man stepped on a nex manz trainers, what do people expect in them shub-in places though, there's no space.

11th March 1997
Woke up at Kim's and we were all still in our clothes from last night, they stunk of weed from the Blues. Later on, Dejuan came to mine with his friend, we were chillin and watching MTVBase.

12th March 1997
Dejuan doesn't go to the same school as me, his is about a 15 min walk from mine, so at dinnertime I went and met him. After school me and Monique went to Midpoint, but I didn't see Dejuan, I wonder if he went to Central Station Youth Club instead.

13th March 1997
Today was dry.

14th March 1997
Went Greenfields school at Dinnertime and saw Dejuan, we've been checkin' for 3 weeks now.

15th March 1997
Went Woodberry Shopping Centre with Monique, I bought a Kickers bag and a Kangol wallet. Saw some of the Hit Squad Crew up there. You never guess who we saw up there, Floyd and Devante, can you believe it? From the day they stood me and Monique up we aint heard from them you know. Floyd was saying how he was sorry and that something came up and how he'd lost my pager number blah blah blah. I didn't have the heart to tell him I was seeing someone else, so I gave him my number, again.

16th March 1997
Floyd phoned me today. Imagine if Dejuan finds out I'm talking to him, fukin hell.

17th March 1997
Lashelle told me that someone told her that Dejuan's got nex gyal. What the fuk, I can't be dealing with this nonsense tonight. Don't know what to believe when it comes to Lashelle though, she tells too many lies.

18th March 1997
Dejuan came down, we lipsed. The cigarette taste was horrible, and I told him. He found it funny. He loves his Embassy No: 1. He said he hates when I eat Tangy Toms or vanilla ice cream Monster Munch and kiss him, so I

shouldn't moan. He's lucky; 'cause my favourite crisps are Petrified Prawns and I aint lipsed him after eating those yet, ha. I asked him 'bout having nex gyal, he said he aint got no nex gyal and that Lashelle's chattin' shit. I believe him.

19th March 1997

I'm gonna write a letter to Monique to see what she thinks about all this.

Yo Monique. It's me Imani. I thought I'd write to you 'cause it's easier than talking face to face, plus this science lesson is dry. It's all this Dejuan business, he's saying he aint got no next gyal. The whole thing is really confusing. He told me that people are talking balls. Lashelle's doing my head in, she's saying she's gonna deny everything if Dejuan asks her, yet she was the one that told me. Lashelle's a shit stirrer and she's trying to get out of all of this. If she denies saying it then it looks like I've just made the whole thing up. Do you think Dejuan's a playah?

I heard that Trayvon had a fight with someone and apparently the boy is on a life support machine, he could be getting done for murder, can you believe he still aint speaking to me since I dissed his stupid cat, it's been like 3 months now. The bang was sweet though!

Oh, and I heard that Caleb's meant to have cut off the man's hand with a machete or something too, but leng didn't ketch him. Anyway, I'm gonna go now, love yah (no I'm not a lemon, I love that you're my best friend) I've been writing this letter all lesson, the teacher is going mad, they can fuk off.

Anyway, in a bit.

20th March 1997
Saw Dejuan, got my lips. I met Monique, we went bus depot and chilled up there, got home at 11pm.

21st March 1997
I had an argument with the   teacher today, fukin idiot, they   wanna moan 'bout me wearing my   trainers, well you tell my mom to get   me some new school shoes, she will   cuss you out. DICKHEADS. Been checkin'   Dejuan for a month now, yeah.

FUK THE TEACHERS!!!!!!!

22nd March 1997
Moms back, think it'll only be for a few days though. She was saying that she's been getting even more bookings recently. I think she's saving up so we can move to a new house. Our house is ok, but I think she wants a bigger one in a nicer area.
Went Woodberry Shopping Centre with Kim and Monique, they got some manz numbers today. One gyal was shouting "Ey fat gyal the one with Imani who thinks she's black, stop wearing cornrows you're white." I turned round and said "listen, don't start nothing, she aint troubled you, she can wear cornrows if she want's." Then the girls started to walk towards us, yooooo, we legged it, ha.

23rd March 1997
Janay told me that Dejuan knocked me, but I wasn't in, can't believe I didn't get to see him.

24th March 1997
Everyone you can think of was at Central Station Youth Club.

26th March 1997
Saw Dejuan (yeahh yeahh) today, he looked tick. Trayvon was at Central Station Youth Club, he's out on bail for that fight he had. I aint seen or spoken to him since the beginning of the year, he told me to call him when I got home, so I did. I know that I shouldn't have 'cause I'm with Dejuan now, but it was just a quick catch up, after all he's the one that's always had my heart. I asked him if he was really beks about me dissin his cat, and if the boy he had a fight with was ok.

27th March 1997
I've heard that Dejuan's meant to have lipsed nex' gyal. This is the second time recently KISS MY TEETH. Well, I'm glad that I *did* call Trayvon yesterday now, all about the back up! FUK Dejuan, he's a DICKHEAD.

28th March 1997
Went to a party today, I'm sleeping at Monique's.

29th March 1997
Nyah was giving me too much joke today. Saw Dejuan today when I was in town, I walked past him, got no time for him, dyam fool.

30th March 1997
Went to another party today, it was dark. I wore a tennis style dress, Dejuan was there, he said I looked nice. I couldn't even be bothered to ask him 'bout lipsing nex gyal, he just tells pure lies.

Caleb was at the party asking every gyal for a shine, the tramp.

1st April 1997

Been on pure bops today, Kim's sleeping at mine, she's asked Janay to cornrow her hair. She nuh learn har lesson from the other day!

2nd April 1997

Dejuan's been with me ALL day. I still aint asked him about lipsing that gyal. We walked passed Imogen's house and he told her I'm his gyal, yeahhh. I felt sweet. Even if he did lips nex gyal at least people know he's with me. Today was dads birthday, I made him a card and got him some aftershave. I thought he'd like the card true I made it myself, but when I went to his house he said that it looked like Chana had made it and couldn't I afford a 'proper' card. I was trying to say that I did have the money, but I thought this one would be nicer to keep. He dashed it down and said it looked like an art and craft project by Neil Buchanan and how I watch too much Blue Peter and Art Attack. I won't get fuk all next time, too ungrateful man.

3rd April 1997

Dejuan was being really nice to me for some reason today, he's probably feeling guilty 'bout all the slags he's supposed to have lipsed. I've enjoyed spending time with him, but I've been thinking about Trayvon today too. What's wrong with me?? But Dejuan is ok, he makes people know I'm his gyal, for example:

- He told Imogen I'm his gyal
- When his cousin asked where he was, he said "*I'm with my gyal, Imani*"
- He walked me to the bus stop and waited for my bus to come

4ᵗʰ April 1997
Got my hair done in plaits, it looks dark.
I've been with Dejuan now for 6 weeks yeahhh.

5ᵗʰ April 1997
Town was ram out today, pure people were up there. Saw Dejuan, got my tingz off him. I'm staying at Kim's tonight. On the way to Kim's, we stopped at the chip shop. As we were about to leave, these girls were blocking the entrance, they said I could go past but Kim couldn't 'cause they heard she's a slag and loves black man, and that the only way past them was if she gave them £3. Kim started looking in her purse like some idiot. I said, "listen she's with me, she aint done you lot anything, leave her alone man." They were like "nah, we want some money from her first." Meanwhile Kim was still there looking in her purse like some fool. I said "no-one aint getting any money, so what then?" The girls started pushing Kim, then the chip shop owner came out from behind the counter and run them away. I can't understand what their problem was. We carried on walking to hers and she was so bummy that they might be following us, but they weren't. She kept saying thank you to me for sticking up for her. She's my friend, I aint gonna let ANYONE take the piss with her. SIMPLE.

7ᵗʰ April 1997
Mom went to Portugal today. Think she's gonna be gone for quite a while, I overheard her on the phone saying that the group has got 10 shows over the next few weeks. Other than that, today was dead. I aint even in the mood to write, just knowing that she's off again is pissin' me off.

8th April 1997
Kim's sleeping over 'again', she wants Janay to try and put some finger waves in the back of her hair. I swear it's like she aint learning her lesson. Dejuan's staying with his dad at the moment 'cause he's been wrenk to his mom and she aint putting up with it anymore.

9th April 1997
Saw Dejuan in town, he came back to mine; we chilled and watched MTVBase. Janay's at work, then she's staying at Alisha's. I wonder if the kids at her workplace have been messing about in the ball pit again!

10th April 1997

 Saw Dejuan about 3 times today, we lipsed. I said, "you've got lipstick all over your mouth!!" He said, "it don't matter, you're my gyal, I aint got nothing to be ashamed of." Jheeze, I felt sweet. His mouth tasted minty. I asked what he'd been eating, he said he'd started to smoke Berkeley superking menthols now 'cause I moaned about the fag taste the other day!

I'm in my room thinking about Dejuan, he's tick still. I wonder what he'll look like in a couple years' time. I remember when there was a rumour going round that he had nex gyal, I was screwing at the time, but he told me I was the only one he wanted and how people chat shit. I knew the rumours were all bullshit.

15th April 1997
Saw Dejuan today, I'm not sure if we are still checkin' 'cause he aint

said much lately. I used the tarot cards that Monique got me for my birthday, and I asked them if I should bang Trayvon behind Dejuan's back, it read:

This card advises you to think very carefully about any decision you have to make. You should consider not only the consequences, but also everything that's happened in the past which has led you to this point.

I guess the cards telling me to loawe it with Trayvon. Monique was telling me that Dejuan's told her that he might finish with me but that he still likes me. I knew he was acting weird lately. She said he sounded confused. Now what am I meant to do? Wait around for him to dun with me?? Fukin hell man. My cards for tomorrow talk about expecting disappointment (isn't it bad luck to read the next day's star sign ahead of the actual day-SHIT?) so I'll probably get dumped tomorrow.

So basically, my cards are telling me not to bang Trayvon and that me and Dejuan are gonna dun. Who will I check now if me and Dejuan dun?

16th April 1997
My star sign for today read:

This card suggests disappointment in love, unhappy endings, and deceit. Don't get too bitter about recent events or you'll end up making yourself very unhappy. Stop thinking of revenge, this is not the answer.

I saw Dejuan at Central Station and he just came up to me and said we aint linkin' anymore and walked off. My horoscopes were right. I should've stuck with the big manz and loawed these little yeutes. It would have been two months if we were still together, I'm beks but life goes on.

Last month I heard that Dejuan lipsed Elanor Marshall. Monique saw her today and asked her and she said yes she did lips him. Little bitch. Probably a good job that me and him are done 'cause I'd FUKIN take off her head right now.

17th April 1997
Big, big fight happened in depot today, apparently Trayvon has bruked up someone. How's he in town fighting and he's already on bail for putting that boy on a life support machine? He doesn't learn. When I tried to phone him to find out if the rumours were true, he had already moved up out the area, he said he was staying away for a bit.

18th April 1997
Monique told me that Dejuan was asking her at school when was the last time she saw me. What's he asking for? He can clear off and carry on lipsing his slags, I'm gonna tell her to tell him not to ask any questions 'bout me.
I'm chilling in my room listening to Usher 'You make me Wanna', I love this track.

19th April 1997
Got a postcard from Nyah today. She's saying she's in America, she must have forgot she told me she's *actually* going to Africa, at least she's keeping up with the lie! She was saying how her uncles funeral was sad and that she's met loads of family she never knew she had. She's got their addresses so that she can keep in contact with them when she gets back home.

21st April 1997
Can't even remember what happened today.

23rd April 1997
Saw Dejuan at Midpoint Youth Club, he said hello. I said hello back. I shouldn't have really; prick, but I still like him though.

25th April 1997
Went to Monique's today, her house is dark. She's got her own bedroom, it's massive. Her shelves are full of pure stuff; a fibre optic lamp, a slinky and a mad collection of marbles too. I'm sure I saw an electronic diary on the shelf too, she's kept that quiet. Her gel pen collection is fat too. She's even got a phone line in her room, she's got a plastic phone, the ones that are see through. Her lip balm collection is heavy, but she aint got that many flavours though. She's got a dream-catcher above her bed; I want one of those man. There's a purple border going round the middle of her room, the top part is painted peach and the bottom is red. It looks dark. She's even got a part in her rooms that is separate for her clothes. Marcia has kitted out Monique's bedroom.

26th April 1997
Lashelle's been pissin' me off today, she's so annoying.

27th April 1997
Monique told me that Dejuan said he was gonna call me, I wonder what for? I wonder if he wants to get back together.

1st May 1997

School was closed today 'cause of the general elections; so, everyone was in town. It was the hottest day of '97'. Bare people were in town with sweat patches on their clothes, madness. Got certain gyal walking round like they're nice and their armpits stunk. Everyone in town was drinking them cheap Panda bottles of fizzy pop. I bought a few Sunny Delights and a couple Mr Freeze tip tops to cool me down. They've bussed a new pineapple flavour, it tastes dark. Some people went corner shop and bought the orange calippo's, they're not tha lique. The juice melts and it leaves bits at the bottom of the packet that you end up sucking out like some shiner, not me star. Some bruk pocket gyal in town were bussin mini milks!

2nd May 1997

Dejuan told Monique that he's thinking of asking me back out, ha, he's funny. BRUTE.

4th May 1997

Monique's birthday today but I couldn't even call her, house phone is on incoming calls till Janay pays the bill. Hopefully, she won't be beks that I never called, plus I weren't looking to walk down there in the rain.

Couple of them lot from school came to mine to revise for the mock exams.

5th May 1997

I phoned Trayvon, he's still outta town, said he's back on the 28th. He sounded tick on the phone. Can't wait for him to come back. He said leng are still looking for him and he aint able to get lock up over all that fighting shit.

6th May 1997

English exams were easyyyyyyyyyyyyy.

Dejuan told Monique to tell me to call him. What for?

7th May 1997

I went Midpoint with Louise. She's my good bredrin still. I aint seen her in ages, she was living with her grandad for a bit, her younger brother hallucinates and Louise can't be dealing with it! She's back at her mom's now. Her hairs grown since the last time I saw her. It's like a gingery brown colour, thick and curly, it suits her. Everyone was in town after school today.

8th May 1997

Moms back from Portugal, finally. I like it when she's back. I phoned Dejuan, he was at home, I finally got to talk to him. He said he had just been talking about me, I asked him who to, but he wouldn't tell me, idiot. Considering he's been begging Monique to ask me to call him, he weren't really saying nuen.

I've been revising from 4pm-6:30pm then again from 10pm-11:30pm. Got a Maths exam tomorrow, I've gotta get better at Maths. If I don't mom will buss my arse. Why do parents expect you to be good at EVERYTHING? I wonder what she got in her exams, ha. My maths teacher has moved me from levels 3-5 to 4-6, he's finally come to his senses! If I put my head down, I should be ok. Its 11.45pm I'm really tired.

9th May 1997
GAYNORS BIRTHDAY

Its 4.50pm, school was hard today man, that maths exam was tough. I heard that Dejuan's friend was slyly listening on the other end of the phone when I was talking to him yesterday. PRICK. Apparently he was gonna ask me back out but he never because he didn't wanna ketch any shame in case I said no.

My head of year; Mr Hanson is a knob (I had on jeans today 'cause my tights laddered and I didn't have anything else to wear) he didn't let me in the exam until 9.15am. I felt shame, everyone was staring at me till I found my seat. I'm gonna go now 'cause I gotta clean up, so I'll write later and tell you the 4-1-1.

Ok its now 1am. Earlier on I went next door to give Gaynor a present and a card that I made for her. She loved it, unlike my dad that time when I made his card. I got her a book called 'The Art of Forgiveness', she needs to forgive her daughter Eileen so that she can see her grandson Charlie. Gaynor said she couldn't wait to start reading it. I chilled round there for an hour, she was asking how I was and how school had been. I told her about the maths exam being solid and that I really struggle with it, she said in her Yorkshire accent *"don't worry Lass, its ok, just continue to aim high you'll do well in life no matter what path you choose..."* I really rate her for that, she's right, I guess. The school put too much pressure on us and me and maths are never gonna be friends. She was saying that when she was a headteacher she told the staff not to stress their students out. I wish she could have been my Headteacher.

10th May 1997

Went to a party with Monique. I drank ½ a bottle of Hooch, a Bacardi Breezer, and some Alize. I got pissed out my face. Me and Monique had to keep going outside to get fresh air. I danced with a few boys and this boy called Elijah. This other boy wanted to dance with me, but Elijah told him I was his girl and to move! I don't know what he was going on like that for, this first time I'd ever met him, strange. I felt bad for that boy, there was no reason for Elijah to act like I was his girl.

I swear I've seen Elijah around before with a girl. I wonder if he's already going out with someone. He asked for my number, I gave it him. He looked nice; dark skinned, a bit taller than me, narrow nose, and thick eyebrows.

Monique got asked out by this boy, his name is Jamar, but he told her to call him Mr Gold Teet. He was saying that he's 18 and that he's got his own place. My man was kriss, golden skin, fresh beard, fresh locks and he had pure gold teeth in his mouth. JHEZEZE.

The party was good. Got home at 1.45am. Mom didn't say anything, thankfully. I looked dark at the party (no, I'm not being big headed). I wore a black bell bottom suit, with shorts underneath; the suit was pure lace. I wore it with a white jacket. Monique wore red pum pum shorts and a black top. I don't wanna go school on Monday, I danced with some of them boys so it's gonna be awkward, Nah, actually it'll be ok, it was only a dance anyway. Oh yeah, Nyah is back from Africa, or America ha! She's so funny.

11th May 1997
Monique told me that one boy was saying that my figure looked sharp in my outfit at the party, and all the girls were saying that I thought I was nice. Jealous bitches.

12th May 1997
I phoned Trayvon; my man sounded tick, we spoke for a bit, then I told him I'd call him back tomorrow. Went Central Station Youth Club, it was ok, loads of people were up there. Elijah, that boy from the party was there, he was giving me joke. He was asking me if I wanted to be his girl. I asked if he was with anyone, he said he's just seeing this girl called Shola, but it wasn't anything serious. He said he would call me tomorrow.

13th May 1997
Them lot at school were being their usual selves (dickheads). Nuff people were in town after school today. Everyone's been chattin' Monique saying how she's a sket. I've been trying to call Trayvon all day but haven't got hold of him.

We heard that Elijah got arrested yesterday and he might get sentenced, no wonder he hasn't called. I wonder if he's going out with that girl, Shola?

14th May 1997
School was joke today. My tights laddered again, (I swear I need to buy more expensive tights) the boys were staring at my legs all day, I don't blame them. My legs are nice. Ha! I phoned Trayvon, he was telling me that he was eating a pizza, garlic bread, nuggets, and a cake, (he's craven) he said when he comes back down in a couple weeks that he's

here for good (yeahh yeahh). He's given me his address so I can write him a letter while he's outta town. I hope he does come back down soon.

Lashelle was doing my head in AGAIN today. Chattin' balls (what's new?) When I was on the phone to Trayvon she tried to make me look stupid and shouted down the phone that I'd been graffitiing his name over my Science book, I had to cover the phone with my hand to stop him from hearing. Trying to bait me up.

I phoned Monique after school but her phoned was engaged, she was probably on the phone to Mr Gold Teet. I'll have to find out tomorrow.

15th May 1997
We all got ketch in the drama theatre at dinner time; it was raining and none of us were looking to go outside in that rain. The teachers were trying to say we 'had to'. Are they mad? Black people and rain don't mix too well, the teachers don't know how long it takes for us to buss these hairstyles, we can't afford for our hair to frizzle and dry out! This time they're all sitting in the warm staff room, nah fuk that. They were saying that we're banned from E block for 2 weeks now (that's what they think anyway). E block is where the canteen is and stuff, so I'd love to see who they're gonna ban from down there.

The school dinners are shit, the best things are the turkey drummers and the pizza slices, and even they're hard and crusty most of the time. But true we're on free school meals we can't just go chip shop. I hate being on free school meals it's so shameful having to line up and wait for them to give you a ticket. The school make it so bait. Don't get me wrong, EVRYONE else is on free school meals too, it's just shameful though man, especially when all the Indian people just breeze past you in the line because they got their OWN money.

Trayvon is my number 1. I've done tings with him 4 times now (I think). I've been linking him off and on since August 95, its now May 97, madness. He's turning 16 next month.

I phoned Monique, she was telling me that she went to Mr Gold Teet's yard yesterday, she couldn't tell me the full details 'cause her mom was in her bedroom hoovering up.

16th May 1997
Everyone at school was saying they're gonna steal food from the canteen. I don't blame them, you can't even get a decent meal with the free school meals. The tokens are worth £1.18, but chips and pizza (without a drink) come to £1, so you always gotta find money to top it up.

17th May 1997
It was Monique's aunties wedding today, I was invited, everyone looked dark. After the wedding I came home and chilled.

Nyah has gone to a Jungle Blues, she asked us to go but I was too tired after the wedding.

It's been a long day; I've been up from 8am and its 11.30pm now. I'm gonna go downstairs grab some food, hol' a fresh and head to my bed.

P.S Mom goes away AGAIN on Monday, I think she's gonna be in Denmark. I can hear her in the bathroom practising her vocals. Part of me wants her to make it as a singer so then she can get paid big money and we can move to a new house, but then another part of me thinks, if she does make it, are we even gonna see her?

But hear tha lique, she's only going for 3 weeks this time, yeah. Normally she's away longer than that. She said that she would bring us back some T-shirts from the tour.

18th May 1997
Today was fuked, and I can't be arsed.

19th May 1997
School was ok, mom went today, I hate when she leaves. We're staying at home with Janay and moms asked her friends Sonia and Gaynor to keep an eye on us.
Oh yeah, today some dickhead tried to reverse the charges to Dejuan's yard, then tried saying they were me. Are they fukin mad, like I'd do that?

20th May 1997
I'm sure Lashelle fancies Trayvon, in fact I don't think, I know. She asked me for his number. I said it was cut off, hear this dickhead "give it me so I can try it anyway." I said "nah loawe it." She sucked her teeth, but she can piss off for all I care. Dickhead. You know how hard I had to work to get this number, you think I'm just gonna hand it to you, mus' be mad.

I got a letter from my pen pal today. I started writing to her when the school set up some pen pal scheme. Me and her keep in touch every now and then, but I aint heard from her in ages. I feel to cut off the stamp and take it to the shop and get 26p for it and buy some sweets with the money (joke). Her letter is sad though man, she's saying that she's started to cut herself 'cause she feels so lonely and like no-one understands her. I get what she means though. I think I should tell someone about what she's said, but who? I don't even know her like that, I've never met her, she's just someone I write to, but I do feel like I know her. Should I tell the school? But she's begged me not to say anything. Nah I'm not gonna go behind her back, I hate when people do that kinda shit to me, so I won't do that. I'll write back and tell her to try and stop or to try talking to a teacher. Actually, I'll ask Gaynor for some advice she'll know what I to do.

Going to bed.

21st May 1997

Today would've been 3 months if I was still with Dejuan. Monique said that she saw him at school and how he told her he's checkin one nex gyal now, but he still likes me, fukin joker. Monique said he's always asking her 'bout me. Ha. Like Aaliyah's tune says, 'if your girl only knew...!'

Went to Midpoint Youth Club today, the Rising Star manz were there too. I got in at 10.15pm.

My days been fuked up, people are getting on mine and Monique's nerves. They chat us and think we don't know, then they try and suck up to you, I'm not havin' none of that. You mad.

A few weeks ago, I asked my dad if I could go to Sweden with the school, he said "of course you can guh, ow much it carst." I told him it was £600, he said that was ok. Today Mrs Kumar was runnin' me down for the deposit money for Sweden, if I fukin had it, she would get it. She needs to cool down. She's one of those Asian teachers that thinks they're white, she really tries hard to fit in. When she first came to the school she used to wear proper Indian suits and stuff which I rated her for, at least she was keeping it real. The bright colours she used to wear really showed off her looks, she's really pretty man. Then all of a sudden she changed, she just became another one of 'them'. We call her 'Mrs', but I swear she doesn't even wear a ring, I'm gonna check next time I see her. My gyals trying to pretend she's married for status!

I went to Sonia's; (moms best friend) for dinner today, when I got to hers I saw a car that looked just like my dad's pulling off, I wonder whose got the same car as my dad, 'cause his cars are exclusive?

22nd May 1997

Yesterday Nyah said that after P.E them lot were saying that I had a wicked figure and how the other girls were getting jealous. After school I phoned Monique, and she was telling me how she wasn't meant to tell me about Dejuan linkin' nex gyal. Who are her loyalties with? It shouldn't be with Dejuan or that big head gyal.

Today we got bigged up nuff times on Ace-1 Radio; they said, "big up Hotness, Frisk-E, Ritch Bitch and Mad Gyal hottest gyal a road right now." Yooooo the whole crew got a mention.

Mrs Kumar was still runnin' me down for the trip money. Why did she shout down the corridor in front of everyone, "Imani when will you be paying the balance?" Do you know how embarrassing that was? I shouted back "**<u>Fuk Knows, I don't work.</u>**" Fukin idiot. She knows she'll get it; she must want my mom to tell her to fuk off. I wish I was able to pay it off in one go like everybody else. I'll phone my Dad and tell him that the payment is due.

Oh yeah, I looked at her hand and there definitely wasn't a wedding ring on it. Maybe she's divorced. Maybe she had to have one of those arranged marriages and now she's bruked free from him. All I know is that it should be Miss and not Mrs. There's definitely something sly about her.

23rd May 1997

I phoned Monique, she was telling me that Dejuan has lipsed Imogen. What's that about, wonder if she takes them stupid braces out when she's kissing people. I can't believe it. No wonder when I was with him she was snooping and asking him if he was 'doing a ting with me,' all along the duti-e gyal wanted him for herself.

Went out today. Nyah decided to go home early, it's probably 'cause her aunty Nzinga gave her a curfew, but she was trying to style it by saying she was tired! It was only 8.45pm, so me and Monique went to Mr Gold Teet's yard.

When we left Mr Gold Teet's; we saw couple of the manz in depot, they were just chillin'. We were talking to them for a bit. We saw Ebony in depot, and she was beggin' for money-that's all she does, it's disgusting, beggy. I only had 25p to get back home and Monique never had any, so we didn't give her anything. All she does is hang around in depot trying to tax us yeutes, she's an idiot. She's a few years older than us and thinks she's a soldier, I aint giving her anything, she needs to find a fukin job, the tramp. She thinks that 'cause she's tall and fat that she can scare people. The only thing scary 'bout her is that black lip liner she wears with the jet black lipstick to match. What does she favour? She looks like an Umpa Lumpa!

I called my dad today; I told him that Mrs Kumar was tryin' to shame me about the trip money, he said "nuh worry me a guh sort it out." He was telling me that him and Nina might be moving. Then Nina came on the phone, hear what she said, "Hi Imani, sometimes I speculate and ponder whether the acquaintances you associate yourself with have your greatest interest at heart?" Speculate, ponder, acquaintances?? Nina fuk off. You aint in Cambridge now. TWAT.

Your own son doesn't even live with you, he lives with his dad; so, you're in no position to be chat to me. I don't blame him. I remember one-time hearing Nina and dad arguing, dad was sayin "how yuh mek de people tek whe yuh pikni?" She was mumbling something about her job being important and she didn't see anything wrong with leaving her son at home while she went to work. Dad told her about herself. If she ever knew that I heard that argument she'd humble herself. It was probably good that her son did get taken off her and went to his dads 'cause Nina probably wouldn't even make him have a burger from McDonalds, she'd probably say 'theres too much sugar and fat' in them, fuk off Nina. Who'd wanna live with someone so dry?

I'm gonna get washed and chill out and watch Club Class, it's a black comedy. It's on channel 5 at 11.40pm and the host is that tick man called Richard Blackwood. (Jheeze). I still can't believe Dejuan has lipsed Imogen. Imogen is slyyyyyyyyyyy. Me and her are nothing alike, does that mean Dejuan goes for anyone, she's geeky and weird and wears that dumb rucksack and dungarees like she's 10 years old, I'm mature, stylish, and way prettier.

24th May 1997
Its 1am, I'm so tired but I gotta write about what's happened today.

After town we went to Mr Gold Teet's house, Monique finally banged him (nuff respec' to her). After we left, she gave me the lingwa. She said it never hurt. Gyal arl-a lie. She had this smile on her face all the way back and she kept laughing to herself, the bang sweeted her!!

Monique was in the room with him from 6pm till 9pm, (3 hours to rarse). Oh, she told me that he said she's got pretty feet. My man's got some foot obsession!!

On the way back we saw Ebony and she was beggin' for money again, that's all she does. When we said we didn't have any, we saw her go over to another set of girls and ask them the same thing. When they said no, she started to check their pockets, I reckon she did that to them 'cause they had a few white girls with them. Ebony can't stand white girls who hang around with black girls, she's an idiot.

25th May 1997

I phoned Trayvon and he was telling me how yesterday he went shopping with his friend and he got himself a Moschino top (his head favour name bran'!!) He said that all charges have been dropped against him so he's ok to come back to the area now! He's coming back on Wednesday.

At school them lot were chattin' Monique, they're outta' order. I tell her most of what they say, I didn't tell her everything because I know she'd be pissed off. Its midnight. I'm going to bed, I'm shattered.

26th May 1997

Jungle party at Shouters Night Club was alright. Loads of people were there. Naomi Smith from Queen Cartel Squad and one nex gyal had a fight. Naomi bruked her up bad. I wonder what it was about. I heard that Naomi scratched up the girls face bad. Madness!!

Nyah was meant to come out today, but she never had any money (what's new).

I went to Gaynor's today. I was asking her what she thinks I should do about my pen pal Kerry Cook and whether I should tell a teacher. Gaynor said that I should say something because cutting yourself is a cry for help and she might even end up killing herself. She told me to tell Kerry to find help and that if she didn't then I'd have to tell someone. Gaynor said that if I ever felt like how Kerry does, then I must come and see her. Gaynor said that the book I gave her for her birthday is making her think about writing to her daughter Eileen, she asked me what I thought. I said I think she should because I know how much she wants to meet Charlie her grandson.

Sonia cooked dinner for us today, she's a good cook to be fair, she dropped off liver and rice with sweetcorn, it was tha lique. She even gave us some tinned stuff to put in the cupboards, she works at Kwik Save and gets us discounts on stuff, moms so lucky to have a friend like Sonia, she definitely makes sure we are ok when moms away on tour.

27th May 1997

Trayvon should be back tomorrow, aint seen him in ages. Everyone's chattin' Monique, the way I see it is that she is very pretty, and people are jealous 'bout that. She likes going out and enjoying herself (when Marcia, lets her!!) and that's why people chat her. She's probably one of the prettiest gyal on road, and when she busses her bucket hats and has her hair out, yo she looks dark, trust me. No, im not a lemon, I just like how she dresses that's all.

The other day I overheard someone saying that they reckon Monique's gonna be a skettel when she loses her virginity (true they don't know she already has!!)

28th May 1997

Today's been ok, Nyah knocked for me at 2pm, (I wasn't even dressed), she said she'd just seen TRAYVON up the road. I got ready soooooooo quick, but by the time I got up there, he'd gone. I was so beks. I can't believe I never got to see him.

Nyah keeps sayin that Monique is taking long to lose her virginity and laughing, I said "don't watch Monique." Dem gyal are fool. Nyah aint even lost hers so I don't know what she's going on like that for.

I'm gonna ring Trayvon tomorrow to see whar gwarn.

When I was in depot, Ebony and her friend were arguing with some girls, Ebony thinks she's bad. She's a fukin bully. Fukin Umpa Lumpa! She walks around like she owns the place. But no-one messes with her. The other girls were runnin' up their gums. Ebony wasn't havin' any of it. She started to push them around. Madness!

At school, Parminder was asking me to help her think of a nickname. How's she askin', 'bout nickname', she's Indian. Anyhow her dad finds out that she's tryin' to look for a nickname! She better go an' read two books, bout nickname.

It's getting late now I'm listening to Ace-1 Radio FM then going to my bed.

Oh, mom phoned today but I wasn't in, can't believe I missed her call man, I wanted to speak to her and ask her how the shows were going. I wonder if she's got us those T-Shirts. Chana will probably wear the T-shirt as a nightie! She's so cute, she walks round with her hair in long cornrows that Janay does for her, she's got long hair true her dad's Jamaican Indian. Lucky.

Dad phoned me today asking why I don't like Nina. Well, he wasn't 'asking', he was sayin' how I **need to show her more respect** etc. I really can't be bothered with her though. I made out like I did like her, not gonna exactly say she's like an old bag and that she's miserable am I? I just think she acts like she's better than everyone, for example she says I shouldn't drink fizzy pop because its 'not good for you' and how its 'extremely dangerous' for me and how I should be drinking natural juices. Who the hell drinks natural, homemade fruit juices, except her? She was even saying that she's gonna stop eating meat and she's gonna tell my dad to do the same. I can't imagine dad following her nonsense he loves his Jamaican food; there's no way he's giving up ackee and saltfish, oxtail, cow foot, goat belly or manish water. But who knows though 'cause to be honest I never thought he would even get married. He's always seemed independent even after him and mom split up. Even with Nina being his wife, I feel like he's single. It's weird. I remember when he told me he was getting married, I was like-WHAT? I didn't think he NEEDED ANYONE. Then I met Nina, this marga, feeble mixed-race woman with sharp cheek bones, the first thing I thought was, dads gonna eat you alive. She spoke so timid and seemed shy. I remember her shaking my hand (like it was some kind of business meeting, fool) but the handshake was sooo sarf, you know them weak handshakes? That made me know she was sarf'. All her features were chiselled, and she had this permanent pout like she thought she was a model. Ha. I see past all that bullshit though, there's something about her. She takes herself way too seriously.

29th May 1997

Today has got to be one of the darkest days this month, I saw TRAYVON. He had on Lacoste ear warmers, metallic glasses, and a red Moschino hoodie. My man looked 'ready'. He looked too stush. Monique still can't believe she's banged Mr Gold Teet, he is the hottest boy on road. Soooooooo many girls like him, trus' me. I can see why she's still in shock though.

I saw Caleb, he said that he heard Monique's got nice feet (only Mr Gold Teet has said that). Does that mean that Mr Gold Teet's been chattin' wha' happened? Do I tell Monique? Fukin' ell. I don't think she'll want everyone knowing.

Caleb was practically beggin' all the gyal dem for a bang today (what's new, tramp)

On our way back from Youth Club we saw The Hit Squad Crew, we were chattin' to them for a bit. Me and Janay had an argument, all 'cause she wanted me to hoover the bedroom and I told her she needed to wait and that it didn't even look that messy. KISS MY TEETH. I told Monique but she didn't get it 'cause Marcia does all her hoovering.

30th May 1997
My day's been long. Dad phoned me at 8.30am to tell me he's coming up to drop me off some money, he said he's going to be outta town for a few days. He's looking for a new house with Nina. Well, they better make sure its big enough to fit all of Nina's make up, designer clothes and perfume in, she don't play when it comes to having nice stuff. She wears pure designer clothes, I'm sure she thinks she looks good. It's like she's trying too hard. Sometimes you'll see her bussin' Prada, but the colours she wears are awful, like greens and browns, she looks like Shaggy from Scooby Doo! She's a knob.

Lashelle knocked me to go Central Station Youth Club but when we got there they said it was closed. At 12.30pm Monique still hadn't reached, we phoned her, and she said she was runnin' late and that she'd meet us in town (her timekeeping is a joke).

I bought some Reebok classics for £30. I owed Janay £6, so I gave that back to her, I don't want her runnin' me down for that in front of people, she don't mind to embarrass me. I bought some hair for £4 and I'm using my last tenner for Riverside Fair tomorrow.

I wrote 'BIG UP TRAYVON' on the wall and Lashelle the stupid bitch dragged him to look. I felt so shame. He smiled, so it wasn't too bad.

I used the tarot cards that Monique got me, they said that I was gonna come into some money, but the dates haven't been bang on, but I did get £50 off my dad today. I'm gonna start reading my horoscopes even more.

When we were walking to Youth Club I saw that car that looks like my dad's near Sonia's. Next time I see dad I'm gonna tell him someone's got the same car as him in the area, he's gonna be beks, he likes to have one-cut stuff.

Caleb was beggin for sex again today. When we ALL said no, he turned around and said, "you're all ugly anyway!" Dickhead.

Its 1am now, Club Classic (Black comedy show) wasn't all that tonight.

31st May 1997
Woke up at 8am and took Chana to the doctors, (she's got a chest infection) Chana was up washed, dressed and ready from early, she's on point. I like that. Her mouth was push up when she saw me strolling out of bed at 7am, she'd been ready from about 6am. Janay couldn't be bothered to take

her; she went out last night with Alisha. After the doctors I came home and went back to sleep.

Woke up in the afternoon and went to Riverside Fair. EVERYONE was there. It was pure joke. This boy called Neo asked Monique out today. After the fair everyone was just hanging around depot.

1st June 1997
Riverside Fair was on again, loads a people were there today. Us lot spent all our money on the 'Waltzers' and the 'Dodgems'. I was begging them gyal to come on the 'Tagada', but they were shook. I was trying to say that it wasn't that bad, it's just us sitting in a circle going round fast. Them lot didn't wanna, true say the ride starts throwing people all over the place, they were bummy. They're dry man.

I posted my letter to Kerry Cook (my long-time pen pal) I hope she writes back.

2nd June 1997
Got my hair done, it looks dark, the way the Nyxon gel holds it down yo it aint moving. That gels strong. I've stopped using my Dark and lovely gel, its leaves pure brown flakes in your hair man. FUK THAT.

I aint seen Trayvon in a while. I've phoned him a few times but he aint been in.

I went to Gaynor's house and straightened up her kitchen and living room. I made her sweet and sour chicken. She gave me £10. She was playing 'Falling in love all over again' by Beres Hammond, the tunes dark though. For a white woman she loves black stuff, she was telling me ever since she moved from Yorkshire that the black people 'round here have really made her feel welcome and she loves everything about us; our food, our music, and our vibes. She's always playing 'Substitute lover' by Half Pint, another big tune. Yes Gaynor, big up yourself.

3rd June 1997

Afterschool I phoned Trayvon, he finally answered. We were on the phone for ages, it's all about the 99* phone box scam. I put 20p in the phone box, when it got to 9p, I pressed 'follow on call', then I dropped a £1 in and pressed 99* and got £1.09p of credit and my £1 back. JHEEZE. I rinsed that for hours! The people who were waiting outside the phone box got pissed off and eventually moved up. When we were on the phone I asked what he had been up to, he told me that he's been linkin' one new gyal. BASTARD. How dare he think it's ok to tell me that so casually, ok so I know I aint with him, but he knows how much I like him.

I saw Kim today, but true I was on the bus, I just waved at her. I saw the Rising Star manz in town. Couple of them were runnin' pure gyal saying how nuff gyal aint got no batty but they beg it! They could never do that to me, you mad. They're outta' order.

4th June 1997

I saw Trayvon in depot, he was telling me how he's got a flat in Newman now, why's he telling me? Isn't he linkin' that gyal anymore?

I heard Kim's saying that I saw her on the bus and that I blanked her, is she mad?? I fukin waved at her. She needs to get her eyes checked. She's telling people wait till she sees me?? She can't do me anything. FOOL. I'm the one that's forever saving her arse from getting buss up! SHE NEEDS TO SETTLE HER SKIN!

5th June 1997
After school I did my homework and then went out at 7pm, I phoned Monique to tell her about the argument I had with Kim in Food Tech today. Everyone in class thought I was gonna fight her. I was, but I wasn't in the mood and she aint worth it. She swears blind that I blanked her. She was trying to run up her gums to me. ME YOU KNOW. I will knock her clart into next week. But I aint looking to get excluded from school either. Why would I blank her when I was defending her the other day? She's mad.

I had to go to school bare legged today, my legs looked ok to be fair (didn't have any tights AGAIN)

6th June 1997
Today has been joke, we went Central Station Youth Club after school.

In depot we saw the Queen Cartel Squad, they were up to no good as per usual; taxing people, smoking weed and actin' like they're soldiers.

There's a rumour going round that Nathaniel (Janay calls him sunbeam, true his teeth are ALWAYS yellow!) has been feeling up Mrs Kumar and now Mr Hanson's found out about it. Its mad if he's done that. You think these teachers won't mind to call the feds; they'll lock Nathaniel up and feel no way. I knew Mrs Kumar was dodgy you know, how you gonna make a yeute feel you up, the little slag. She aint married a rarse. Narsty gyal, I bet she loved him touching her up, maybe her husband (if she's even got one) don't feel her up, that's why she comes to school and gets her little rub up.

When I was speaking to Monique earlier she was saying she might loawe Mr Gold Teet 'cause he's fukries and has been chattin' what they did to bare people.

7th June 1997
At school today I had to see Mr Hanson 'cause I wore my stretch jeans instead of my school trousers. My trousers had a rip in them, and my stretch jeans were all I had. They're lucky I didn't skive off, it's a pair of jeans, they're acting like I came in battie riders! They think school's the penn. They think they can chat to me how they want, are they mad? Teacher or no teacher I will tell you 'bout your clart, I don't care.

When I was on my way to Sonia's to drop off Chana, I bumped into my dad. He said that he was just on his way to see me, strange 'cause normally he would phone first. I was telling him how I seen someone else with the same car as him the other day, he was asking me where the car was, who was in it etc, and how his car is the only one in the area. When I told him I saw the car round here, near Sonia's, his face kinda changed and he started to say how he knows one man from back in the day who always copies him, Paul, and how he thinks it could be him.

8th June 1997
Been chilling in my house today listening to Aaliyah's tune '4-page Letter', I've rinsed it about 100 times. I went to

Monique's house today too, I even bought my slippers with me, I didn't need to because when you step into her house, they've got a basket full of slippers still in their packs for people to wear. Marcia aint playing, she doesn't want anyone mashing up her tiled floors! Their house is nice, but I don't know why they've got plastic covering all over the chairs, that's what my nan and grandad have and Marcia aint nowhere near as old as them.

9th June 1997

Jordan's been giving me joke, quite a few people have told me that he fancies me. He's just a school friend though, I wouldn't go out with him.

Monique knocked me at 6pm then we went to Mr Gold Teet's. He wasn't even in, from there we walked up to Central Station Youth Club, couple people were there. Mr Gold Teet was there he actually looked a bit ruff to be honest, hardly recognised him, he blanked Monique. No manners.

10th June 1997

We were playing truth or dare at school and Jordan said he would give my figure an 11 outta 10, Jheeze.

Nathaniel's a knob, he was doing my head in, he thinks he's a big man. Everyone's been asking him what's going on with him and Mrs Kumar, he said that he'd been feeling her up for ages and that she was ok with it, but this time another teacher saw, so Mrs Kumar had to gwarn like she had been 'inappropriately touched'. A wha de rarse a gwarn? He said he's waiting for a meeting or something.

Them gyal were going on so immature today, they don't seem to realise we are in year 9 now, no time to be acting like fools.

11th June 1997

Monique lipsed Neo today. After the way Mr Gold Teet acted the other day like they were strangers, I don't blame her.

Jordan told me I looked tick in my P.E Kit today. He's a joker.

12th June 1997

Moms back, at last. She's still got loads of shows down here but at least she's back in the country. I've finished my homework about the life of Hitler. They never teach us 'bout our black history, like the life of Hitler is something we should be proud of. KISS MY TEETH.

Monique was telling me that her and Neo are proper checking now, so that's good. Neo might go to hers tomorrow, Marcia's going to a women's rights march. At school me and one boy were flirting with each other to get Jordan beks and it worked, it was so funny. Jordan wanted to fight him. I had to tell him to stop being stupid. Jordan going on like I'm his gyal. FOOL.

13th June 1997

It's two weeks until I go to Sweden, I can't wait. I saw Dejuan at Youth Club, I asked him what was going on between us and if he still liked me, he said he'd speak to me later. Later on, we went over to the park. The park was grimey; pure used condoms on the floor and whole 'eap of empty White Lightning Cider bottles lying around the place. We were talking about things, he seemed surprised about how much I knew 'bout the slags that he's meant to have been sleeping with. He said it was all lies. He wanted to kiss me, but his breath smelled of cigarette. We've decided to give things another go. How long for this time, I wonder?

I'm going now, Club Classics is on channel 5.

14th June 1997

Today I saw Dejuan he's been giving me joke. I went to town and got some tie-dyed stretch jeans and some new underwear. Town was dry, no one was there probably because it was raining. I've bought dad a set of drinking glasses and a card for Father's Day tomorrow. I wonder if they'll match the kitchen design in his new house. Nina better not drink out of them either. They aint for her. I remember one time going there for Sunday dinner, my woman served some three-course meal for me her and dad, why is she sooo extra? She did prawn vol au vents, some homemade vegetable Kiev's and roast potatoes which she said she cooked in some fancy oil. They tasted like ordinary potatoes to me! Then pudding was a choice of Eton mess or apple and almond meringue, I told her I didn't like any of them. She rushed out to the shops and said she'd get me a nice dessert, so I'm thinking great; some ice cream or a caramel sundae. Nope, fool fool Nina came back with brandy snaps dusted with cinnamon and nutmeg. You can tell no kids live with her. WHA' the fuk am I doing with brandy snaps, bitch I just want something simple. She aint got a clue. I left it same place on the plate. Ediat. Dad didn't eat it either, he said "me nuh know why yuh a cook arl dat, me just want some curry chicken and some oxtail with rice and peas and a Guinness Punch."

Me and Monique are runnin' a competition to see who can stay with their man the longest. Me with Dejuan and her with Neo.

Janay's gone out and moms got another show tonight. Chana's at Sonia's house. So, I've got the house to myself. Monique was telling me she's going to Neo's tomorrow, we were deciding whether she should bang him or not, we figured she may as well!

15ᵗʰ June 1997
Things that have happened
- Monique went to Neo's,
- I phoned Dejuan, he wasn't in
- Today was National Cinema day and all shows were £1, we went cinema but still couldn't get in, the queues were mad.
- Nathaniel's waiting for a court date for that thing with Mrs Kumar.

16ᵗʰ June 1997
Nobody's chattin' to Nathaniel 'cause he's been chattin' balls 'bout everyone. He's a goofy, dry head, crusty kneecap, sweaty arm pit, yeute bwoy, with a capital B for Bwoy. He's confused, feeling up teachers to rarse, I don't know what's going on with him. Them lot got caught with weed and rizla at school today. Jordan had the most on him, so he's definitely gonna get kicked out, it's the second time he's been ketch with it. Schools gonna be dry without them lot there.

I saw Dejuan today he looked lean up, what's new? Me and Monique went Youth Club today, we kept getting bigged up on the mike, is that how you spell it, actually its mic' as in microphone, my spelling is crap.

Janay said that Floyd called me when I was out. I aint spoke to him since March, I wonder what he wanted me for?

17th June 1997
Monique said that she's seen a picture of that gyal that Trayvon's supposed to be with, and she looks like she's got some kinda illness, her skin's blotchy and pale, and she had yellow spots all round her mouth and eyes, she's probably a shiner. She don't sound all that at all. What's Trayvon playing at? I'm finally getting over him anyway, I never thought I'd ever say that.

Mom went to perform at another show, so I've got the house to myself so I'm gonna chill in with Chana. She's using the hairbrush and pretending to be the main singer from En Vogue, she tried to hit that high note 'don't let go', she sounds ok though you know.

Janay's gone to Alisha's.
Dejuan was meant to call me, but he hasn't, I aint calling him either, aint runnin' him down.

18th June 1997
Went doctor's to see 'bout the bumps on my arms (it could be eczema), I never went back to school in the afternoon. Me and Monique met up at Youth Club, she's told Neo to go to hers because Marcia's going to another protest.

Dejuan was telling me he got arrested yesterday for teefing a moped, that's why he never came up to see me.

Lashelle was runnin' Monique to me today saying how Neo is ugly, Lashelle is jealous. She needs to find a man and stop watching people.

My hair needs doing, I'll probably do it on the weekend.

House phone is cut off again, I told Dejuan it'll be back on tomorrow. I asked if his phone was BT or Cable, he said BT. I told him that cable to cable is free. He said, just tell your mom it's cable. Is he mad, so when the bill comes, what do I do then, I aint able to get clap up. Looks like phone box a run.

19th June 1997

My house phone is back on and we've got cable now too. Dejuan's been kicked out of his school for teefing that moped, what's that got to do with school? It wasn't even on their premises, some joke ting.

I'm gonna call Floyd back tomorrow and see what he wanted me for the other day, strange that he's called me after so long.

Louise told me that one gyal she knows asked her, "who's Imani checkin?" listen, tell that gyal to mind her business. Does she fancy me or something, 'bout she's asking who I'm checkin', is she a lemon? When Louise asked her why she was asking 'bout my business, she said it's 'cause she's heard I'm going out with Dejuan and Trayvon at the same time, gyal mind your business.

20th June 1997

Dejuan was begging me to give him some money before I go to Sweden, he's a knob. What the fuk do I look like? I asked him if he's gonna miss me when I go, he said yeah.

I called Floyd today, but his dad said he was out playing football.

21st June 1997

Woke up at 1pm, dad phoned me beks 'cause I never got Nina anything for her birthday. Acting like I'm meant to know HIS wife's birthday. KISS MY TEETH, but seriously Imani how did you forget her birthday! I can't afford the stuff she likes anyway, where am I meant to find the money for Ruby and Millie make up and that aint even her favourite. And I definitely can't afford Lancôme Poeme.

I asked dad what he got her; wait for it:....can we get a drum roll please...he said he bought her some stuff from the Jean Paul Gaultier's Spring collection, (spring collection you know) and some Tom Ford loafers, and I guess for good measure he chucked in the yoga mat and some lotions and potions. Her kitchen's like a medicine shop, pure potions and shit.

Nina doesn't trust the doctors, so she makes her own healthy stuff. She says "Doctors are in business with the pharmacists and that they benefit financially by prescribing medicines as they've got shares and investment in the companies." I remember listening and all I kept thinking was who says pharmacists, it's a fukin chemist! You can tell she's from Cambridge. DICKHEAD.

Why would doctors try to make their patients take tablets if they didn't need to, Nina's a knob, 'bout they've got shares in the chemists. IDIOT.

Nyah and Lashelle had an argument today, but Lashelle was going on wayyyy too extra true Dwayne was there, she was just trying to show off. It's so obvious that she fancies him. I heard that Dwayne's definitely going out with Natalie, so Lashelle better know what she's doing. If Natalie hears that Lashelles trying to move to Dwayne, it's gonna be madness.

I phoned Floyd today, but his dad said I'd just missed him, he'd gone ice skating. I aint gonna keep calling him. He must know what he wanted me for if it's important he'll call me back.

22nd June 1997
I've stayed in my yard all day. I caught some joke on the phone with Monique. After we finished on the phone I was playing Bamboozled on Teletext. It's so annoying 'cause if you get one answer wrong it takes you right back to the beginning, some joke ting. Chana spilt some juice on the remote the other day, so the buttons are sticky, when I was trying to use the red, yellow, green and blue 'fastext' buttons, to choose the right answer it was taking wayyy longer 'cause I had to press the buttons really hard. Chu.

I phoned Trayvon today to say happy birthday, we were chattin' for a bit. Even though we aren't together we do still get along.

23rd June 1997

Things that have happened today

Phoned Monique we were bussin' joke on the phone

- Dejuan phoned me
- I saw Trayvon
- My hair looked nice
- Mrs Kumar was doing my head in about the last payment for Sweden. My dad gave her some the other day and now she's asking for more, yo chill bitch
- I've been listening to pure tunes today.

24th June 1997

Today's been dead. I aint seen Dejuan since Saturday. I've stayed in all day, in fact it's the 3rd day in a row that I've been in my house (not the Lique). I took some photos of us lot at school; can't wait to get them developed, its gonna take about a week to get the pictures back though. I could've got them done on the 2 day return but that was way too teef, so I told the woman I'd go for the 5 day option instead.

I need some money to go to Alton towers for the school trip, everyone's going.

I wanna see Dejuan before I go to Sweden too. What's he gonna do without me for a week, anyhow I hear he's done a ting with them slags; I'll go mad, so he better hold it down till I get back.

25th June 1997

I phoned Monique today. She was telling me that she's getting her room redecorated, it's gonna look wicked. It already does. I wonder what she's going to have now? I think she's gonna go for the stars and moon look, it's blue wallpaper with gold stars and moons on it. Everyone's got that wallpaper, but I know Monique will go all out with the matching bedsheets and the matching lamp.

26th June 1997

It's been pissin' down with rain all day. I phoned Monique, I told her that I'm kinda talking to Kim again now and how she apologised for runnin' up her mouth. I don't really wanna chat to Kim that much 'cause 1) she's a skettel 2) she tells pure lies 3) she chats everyone's business.

Dejuan came and seen me; he was here till 11pm. We've arranged to meet up at Youth Club tomorrow, he said he's gonna be late 'cause he's got a football match. I've only just realised that your man can be like your best friend, but a male version. I think that's what me and Dejuan are like. He was saying that Lashelle should be careful 'bout linkin' Dwayne 'cause Natalie will take off her head. I aint telling Lashelle fuk all, she acts like she's dark, let's see what she's gotta say when she bucks up with Natalie.

I've paid my Sweden trip money, finally. Fuckers can get off my back now.

27th June 1997

Today Lashelle got bummy 'cause Natalie came down the school looking for her, but Lashelle had double detention so Natalie didn't wait around. Monique's staying here tonight, oh yeah she had to take the emergency pill today. Madness. We've heard that Neo; her man, has banged nex gyal.

Dejuan was giving me joke today, he was so happy that he won his football match.

We heard today that Trayvon isn't seeing that gyal with the blotchy skin anymore and that he's meant to be doing a ting with L'Neisha. She's originally from Jamaica, I think, but she's moved here to live with her dad, I heard her mom died or something in a car crash out there. The gyal aint even been here two minutes and she's already tacking up man! She's really pretty, she's dark skinned and her figure is mad. Every time I see her, she's wearing something tight fitting and her breasts are on show.

28th June 1997

I went Woodberry Shopping Centre today. I bought a top from Tammy Girl. If you aren't quite ready for Morgan, then Tammy Girl it is! On my way to Woodberry, I saw Nina, she gave me £100, I couldn't believe it. She just pulled it out of her purse. I asked what designer her purse was (you could tell from the stitching that it was designer) she said it was some Australian designer called 'Helmut Lang'. She's a joker you know, bout Australian designer and here's me getting excited about going into C&A! C&A didn't really have anything, so I went straight into 'The Sweater Shop'. I bought a Fruit of the Loom jumper. I even got some stuff from Our Price, normally when I go in there I just look at all the tapes, but not today, yooooo I bought pure tunes. Music collection's looking fat. Went into Woolworths and grabbed a pick 'n' mix, it came to £9 but I didn't mind 'cause I had money today. Oh yeah, went into Beatties and sprayed up some perfume and walked out, not looking to pay their teefin prices for no perfume!

Gonna put £20 in the bank. Might give Chana and Janay a tenner each.

5th July 1997

It's been a while since I've wrote in here, I've been to Sweden with the school, it was good. I took bare pictures of the forests and lakes, we even went on a ferry to Stockholm, it was alright still. I can't wait to develop my camera film; I took some wicked pictures. I saw Dejuan today he said that he missed me when I was away, I told him that I bought him a little present he was dying to know what it was! Mom's in Bristol she's got 3 shows to do this weekend, she's gonna be shattered man. I don't know how she does it. I've hardly seen her since I've come back.

6th July 1997

Today's been ok, I phoned Dejuan, but he wasn't in. Mom came back home at 11pm with a proper attitude, don't know why. What happened to the shows? Have they been cancelled or something? I didn't even ask her. Wonder if she's fallen out with some of the other backing singers?

7th July 1997

Saw Dejuan today. He had his arm round me all day. I felt sweet until the part when he was asking me to give him some money. What do I look like, he should be giving me money!

Monique went to Woodberry Shopping Centre with her mom today, she bought some purple stretch jeans.

8th July 1997

I heard Jordan's saying he likes Parminder and how she's pretty for an Indian girl and she's got a big batty. Pretty yeah... batty no!

I can't believe it's been a year since the attempted kidnaping ting at Chana's school with that mad woman. Still mad to think that Chana was there at the time. I wonder if Chana still remembers that day.

9th July 1997

Dejuan came down after school. Monique banged Neo today, she doesn't believe that rumour going around about him with next gyal. Bwoy. A date's been set for Mrs Kumar and Nathaniel's hearing about the touching up ting, but apparently Mrs Kumar is leaving the school and has withdrawn her statement. WHAT THE HELL. She's leaving you know. Are you gonna tell me this woman wasn't loving the little touch up? It was another teacher that saw it so I wonder if the case will still go ahead? Nathaniel's buzzin' that the whole thing has fallen through, he's telling people how he's got her number and that he's gonna still link her outside of school.

10th July 1997

Today I woke up and decided that I'd try and get back in touch with Floyd, it's still bugging me what he wanted me for the other day. I phoned him but his dad answered the phone asking me how close I was to Floyd and one bag of questions. I was thinking what's with all the questions, then he told me that Floyd had died on the pavement outside his house, some postcode beef. I don't think I believed it at first. I've been thinking about him all day.

We've arranged to go to the funeral next week, his dad was telling us the details.

I've heard that Dejuan's got nex gyal in the Fellow Fields area. I phoned and asked him, he said he aint got no gyal down there, but he's heard someone down them sides is supposed to like him.

R I P Floyd

11th July 1997
I heard that Nathaniel's going round saying that Dejuan told him that when we bang I act shy and nervous. Wait till I see Dejuan. Do not chat anything to your little trampy friends.

12th July 1997
Woke up at 1.20pm. I cleaned the house and then Monique and them lot came up. Saw Trayvon today he told me he's checking L'Neisha. He was saying that her yardie accent was strong, but he loved it 'cause it made her sound sexy. How does an accent make you sound sexy, fool?

I wonder if he was trying to say that *I'm not sexy*. I aint anyway.

Its 1.45am I'm tired.

13th July 1997
It's been a month today that I've been checkin Dejuan. It's gone quite quick. I told Dejuan that Nathaniel's going around telling people how he said that I act shy when we bang, Dejuan denied saying that to Nathaniel. Hmmm,

I'm not sure if I believe him. I told Dejuan that he better not chat to Nathaniel again otherwise me and him are dun. He said OK. He knows!

14th July 1997
Janay's gone Club Peach.
I phoned Monique today, she was telling me that she's going to Neo's tomorrow.

15th July 1997
Monique went to Neo's she told me that she banged him. I stayed in today. I'll definitely be going to the Queen Cartel party on Saturday everyone will be there.

I HATE SPORTS!!!

Sports day tomorrow and no one can be arsed. I hate sports day. I wonder if teachers ever feel bad for making us do stuff, I'd hate to be a teacher. I wanna be a Nurse, well I think I do anyway. The idea of helping people is what I like about it. In fact, I'll ask Gaynor, she'll tell me what I need to do.

Kim's a little bitch, she's gone down Monique's today chattin' a bag of lies and shit. I knew I should've stopped talking to her for good. It aint even been two minutes since I've started talking to her and she's already causing trouble. Look how I helped that gyal and now she wants to call up my name.

16th July 1997
I came 4th in the 100 meters for sports day, not too bad I suppose. I was mash up after the race though plus I was thirsty too; the teachers just wanna hand out cheap water

wash orange squash with no flavour. I know they're trying to ration and are always going on 'bout the school budget, but fuk me, the squash tasted shit. Lashelle won the 200 meters and now she thinks she's a fukin athlete, idiot. Dejuan's starting to piss me off, he never calls at the time he's meant to and he's getting a bit dry. He needs to buck up his ideas I swear.

17th and 18th July 1997

Went to Floyd's funeral today, it was so sad. There were pictures of him all 'round the church, the baby ones of him were cute though. All the old people were clapping and playing tambourines dressed in black. You know you're at a funeral when they start to sing 'weeping may endure for a night, but joy comes in the morning'. That's the same dry ass song they sing at everyone's funeral. They better not sing that at my funeral. Ha. When I was looking through the funeral programme there was a picture of him holding a baby. I thought it might be his cousin or nephew or something, but when his best friend Devante started to give the eulogy, he said "Floyd leaves behind a young son..." my heart sunk. A young son. I know nothing ever happened between me and him, but we spoke enough for him to mention he had a fukin son, what's that about? Oh, and he was 19 not 17. Imagine it's at the manz funeral I'm hearing his age and about his pikni, I couldn't believe it.

After the eulogy, the pastor said people could view the body; two at a time. I felt sick. It didn't even look like him in the coffin, it was more like a dummy version. The whole thing took ages, black people funerals are always a long ting. I don't know why we thought we were gonna go back to school in the afternoon; what with about ten different people giving prayers, about three different pastors and his aunt Grace hogging the microphone and going on for ages; (even when Pastor Williams said they had to be quick) there was no way we were getting back to school for 12. Thankfully, at the end of the service, they played Puff Daddy and Faith Evans, 'I'll be missing you'. A tune that us lot knew. I was crying my eyes out man. At the end we followed the casket out of the church behind his family. I just couldn't believe he was in the coffin.

Saw Dejuan today, he was asking if I think it would be better if we just see each other instead. Where the hell has that come from? He wasn't really asking me; Hear how he dropped it:

Dejuan- "I'm gonna ask you something, but don't get beks"
Imani- "Ok ask me then"
Dejuan- "Do you think it'd be better if we just see each other, things aint working out are they?"

(I wondered...Is that a question or a statement?)

Imani- "Err I aint bothered"
Dejuan- "It's up to you"
Imani- "I don't know."

I asked him to go and told him I'd speak to him tomorrow. I'll tell him rago that I want to check him, no sharing man business.

R I P Floyd

19th July 1997
Went to carnival today with them lot, everyone was there. Dejuan was there, he had on the Charlotte Hornets T-Shirt I bought him back from Sweden. How you gonna wear the top that I got you a day after telling me you don't wanna be with me? PRICK. Monique's caught pure man at carnival today, at least 8 man have chatted her up. Neo really better not be slagging it out 'cause Monique was on fire today bwoy. She can have any man she wants!

20th July 1997
The Pop Man didn't turn up today so I went to the corner shop to grab a bottle of Dandelion and Burdock and a bottle of Ice Cream soda. When I looked up the road I saw that car that looked like my dad's again near Sonia's. I was trying hard to see if there was anything different between them, I couldn't remember dad's registration, but I knew it has a D7 in it and so did this one. Surely his friend Paul wouldn't be so fuked up to copy the registration plate.

21st July 1997
Today in assembly, the teachers announced that Mrs Kumar 'wouldn't be with us for the next academic school year in September' and that she was moving on to a school that was closer to where she lived. Everyone in the lecture theatre just started laughing, we all know the 'real reason' she's leaving, nasty slag. The school didn't even get her any flowers or a card, that's how you know she aint leaving on nice terms, they want her out just as much as she wants to leave.

Period pains are killing me, I'm in no mood. Going to my bed.

22nd July 1997
I heard that one gyal from my school called Brianna lipsed Dejuan when I was with him; but they're both denying it. Brianna's a bit trampy; her whole family are a bit bruk down. They don't seem like they have much. Her hair is long, but she just leaves it out, why doesn't she style it?

Went to Alton Towers today, the rides were proper, we caught pure joke. We went on the Black Hole and the Corkscrew, them lot were bummy. They're jokers, that shit wasn't even scary. I handled those rides like a soldier.

28th July 1997
Bwoy I've got some catching up to do, I aint wrote in here for a while.

Monique's seeing someone else 'cause she heard that Neo was doing' a ting with one slag called Vicky. It's not the first time we've heard 'bout this slag. We saw him in depot, and him and Monique had one massive argument. Put it this way, Monique won't be seeing him again and the black eye she gave him, Vicky probably won't want him either.

Lashelles half-brother has come down for the school holidays; his name is Bryson. Everyone was saying that Monique was pushing up herself on him. Lashelles told him that she's a skettel and that he shouldn't check for her. She even lied and told him that Monique's got herpes you know. When Monique asked Lashelle, she denied it, I swear Lashelle's a knob.

 I went Shouters Night club; I can't believe I passed for an 18-year old.

I need to go to Gaynor's to do some ironing, she's been asking for a while, but I've been busy.

I saw Kim yesterday my gyals steppin' up in the world. She looked kinda decent. Her hair looked dark and her outfit was ok still plus she had on some new trainers and a sick puffer jacket. She was still trying the half patois, hear her 'wha gwarn Imani'!! I don't know what she was trying. She asked me if I wanted anything from the shop, I said that I was ok. She pulled out a £50 note and put down a pack of jelly tots and a dib dab on the counter. Mr Singh said he couldn't take the money 'cause it was Scottish and not English. Kim tried to argue with him, but he told us to get out the shop before he sets the dog on us.

29th July 1997

Went next door to Gaynor's with Monique, I did some ironing and got paid £15. Gaynor was asking what I'd been up to and how comes I hadn't been round, I felt bad to be fair. I filled her in on the latest and she listened, all she said was *"Imani, I know you're a young lass and having fun just make sure you are careful and are using protection, the same goes for you too"* she said looking at Monique. Fair play, at least she's asking us yah get me. She said if I ever wanted to talk to her that I must just knock her door. She said she'd been looking at what I need to get in my GCSE's to be a Nurse. She said that I needed to pass Maths and Science and that I would need to go to college or sixth form to do A-levels. She said I'd then need to go to university for three or four years to do a degree, that all sounds long. Don't know if I can be arsed.

We saw Bryson (Lashelles half-brother) today, we took some pics, I hope they come out nice once I get them developed.

30th July 1997

Nothing major has really happened today. Monique never came out, she's taking her hair out. Saw Queen Cartel Squad in town, with spliffs hangin' out their mouths, they think they're bad!

31st July 1997

Today was dry. Monique got her hair done; she looks way younger now than when she had the plaits in! I hate going to hers in the Summer 'cause if I sit on her chairs too long my legs just stick to the rarse plastic like glue. Marcia needs to dash whe that plastic. Only old people have plastic on their stuff.

1st August 1997

Jades staying over, her mom is training to be a Nurse and she has to do mad shifts at New Way Hospital, so mom said Jade can stay here with us on the days her mom does the shifts. Her mom and my mom are good friends, so now we're the shelter house for the needy, I don't know why mom said yes. I asked Jade's mom about getting into nursing, she said the pay was crap and that she wouldn't recommend it. Talk about fukin up my idea. Why's she going into something that she hates?

No-one is chattin' to Nyah 'cause of the lies she's been telling.

2nd August 1997

Today I got my photos back from the ones I took in Sweden, they looked wicked. Monique bought that denim swinger jacket that everyone wants, it looks nice, she bought another bucket hat today, they really suit her. Another carnival is on tomorrow, we might pass up there.

When I was walking past Sonia's house to drop off Chana, I saw dad, he gave me £20 to bring to carnival tomorrow, he said that he's found a house now, so he'll be moving soon. Nina was driving the car today, she had on Prada sunglasses, bright red lipstick and her nails painted in red to match, she looked ok I suppose. Last time I saw her she was driving an Alpha Romeo 146, black of course, all leather interior, the full works. She even had a private reg NIN1. She was telling me to be *vigilant at the parade*. It's a carnival, not a parade I thought! You aint in Cambridge now. She was asking if it's really somewhere that I should be going. Listen, don't try an old me off, I aint 50 years old. I'm going to that Carnival Nina.

Bryson likes Jade (me nah seh nuen). Jade's staying over at ours *again*. She may as well move in! I wonder when her mom's course finishes, I don't mind her staying but she does my head in sometimes.

3rd August 1997
Today we all went Carnival. Nyah got one skeet's number. Jade was saying she thinks Bryson is 'lovely', who says lovely? She's an idiot. Acts like she's posh because her mom's training to be a nurse. Idiot.
Big up Nyah for getting that manz number, big up yourself.

4th August 1997
Its 11.25pm and Jade is sleeping for the 4th night in a row (actually mom said she's gonna be sleeping here for a couple of weeks). Bryson was trying it with me today, but I'm sure he's doing a ting with Jade. JOKER.

5th August 1997

Guess what? I'm going to Jamaica on the 12th September with my dad and Nina. They're going for 2 months, but I'm just gonna go for 3 weeks, I can't wait. Dad's from Trench Town, he said it's in a place called St. Andrews in Kingston. Dad told me that back in the day Trench Town was known as the 'Hollywood' of Jamaica. He was saying that I'll love it and that he's gonna take me to see his brother and sisters who live there that I've never met. Considering dad's been over here for so long his accent is still strong.

I aint really trying to be up and down with Nina so they better not be thinking this is some bonding session. I'll be doing my own ting out there. Dad was saying how he's booking three rooms. Why three? We just need two. I swear he moves funny; I get the feeling he aint really inna Nina. She must have some other uses to him. Who goes away with their wife and has separate rooms, musi mad?

Mind you, the way she looks afraid to speak up, what can she really say to dad! What he says goes, everyone knows that.

Theres a party on next week Thursday at Shouters, its 8pm-1am and its £3 to get in. There's gonna' be Ragga, Soul, Jungle and Hip Hop, think I might go.

10th August 1997

Aint wrote in here for like 5 days. It's 11.56pm and I'm so tired it's unreal. In the last few days quite a bit has happened. Bryson wants to link Monique and he's getting bored of Jade. I aint sure 'bout that one, think you can just move from one gyal to the next, these man are jokers.

Johnathon (Alisha's man) has got a photo of me (I don't know where from), but he came up to me today saying my legs look nice in the photo. Them manz think I'm 15, ha it's so funny. Don't know why he's looking at my legs and he's with Alisha though?

I saw most of Hit Squad Crew in town, them manz are funny. They were saying that they're gonna stop calling themselves 'The Hit Squad Crew' 'cause when one of them does something hot they all end up getting in trouble from the feds.

11th and 12th August 1997

I went to Shouters. EVERYONE was there. Went swimming with Lashelle and Jade, it was ok. Jade thought she was nice today; she always wears her hair out, but after swimming it was shrivelled and looked dry. I don't know why she didn't plait it up like everyone else did. I would love to be able to swim in the sea in Jamaica when I go with dad and Nina, it aint about bussin arm bands. The other day Nina was saying she would teach me, errr no thanks. Why she beggin fren' with me all the time. I have no interest in her you know. She then turned to dad saying, *"wouldn't it be terrific if all three of us went into the sea and took a magnificent photograph and had it framed for the mantel piece."* (I was trying to hold back the laughter when I heard the word 'terrific' and 'magnificent'). Hear dad questioning her; *"sea??, me nah go inna no sea, me a meet mi old friends dem, you nah guh really see mi."* She must have in her head the perfect family holiday, this time dad's looking to meet up with his old friends when he's out there! I wish I could have taken a picture of her face. She was saying that she really wanted to go to the Bob Marley

Museum and the Trench Town Culture Museum, hear dad; *"after me a nuh tourist!"* It was so funny. Nina needs to remember that Jamaica is dad's home, he aint going there like a tourist!

13th August 1997

I saw Mr Gold Teet, he was saying that since he's banged Monique she thinks she's too nice and how she thinks that she can bang anyone. He's a DICKHEAD. I heard that Elijah that boy I met at that party in May is outta Prison now, I wonder if he'll be at Shouters tomorrow. I wonder if he's with that girl he was seeing, Shola?

14th August 1997

Me and Monique went Shouters. It was Ok. Nobody was really dancing. Everyone was round the sides as per usual. Can't believe I saw Elijah, he was telling me that he got lock up for 3 months for some foolishness, he never said what it was though! We were talking for ages outside of Shouters. I asked him about Shola again and he said it wasn't anything serious and that he aint really interested in her. He asked me and Monique if we wanted to go back to his friend's house, so we did. We were all there chilling and watching MTV Cribs'. At 2.15am, me and Elijah went upstairs. (well, you know what happened!) His friend dropped us back home afterwards. Monique slept at mine. We got in at 3.45am. We got pure CUSS.

We were meant to be in at 1.30am. My mom phoned leng, my dad and Marcia too. Why did she call DAD? GREAT, thanks mom! When I was with Elijah he kept talking 'bout living each day like it's your last and how we aint gonna live forever, he was saying how I'm lucky 'cause not many

gyal get to hang out with him and how nuff gyal would like to be in my place. Pleaseee, he thinks he's all that.

15th August 1997

It's Chana's Birthday today, so I bought her another Tamagotchi.

I went to Youth Club, I phoned Monique (because of yesterday my gyal cyar come out a rarse) ha. I gotta go with dad tomorrow to see his new house, not tha lique. Nina was asking me if I'd like to live with them outta town, errr nope! Is she mad? I'd be drinking water and eating grass if it was down to her. Nina, your own son don't wanna live with yah, what makes you think I would? Living with her would be the worst thing ever.

16th August 1997

According to my Horoscopes:
My 'loved up' day is 11th September
My 'listen to my heart' day is 22nd September
I went to Gaynor's to do some ironing, when I was there she was blasting out Sandra Cross's tune 'Country Living,' the tunes a classic. Mom plays it on a weekend when she's cleaning up too.

Johnathon, (Alisha's man) and this other boy came up, they're from outta town. Johnathon was hugging me up and asking me what I'm saying. I told him that it would be stink on Alisha if me and him were to do a ting'. He said she acts childish and how she thinks she's going out with him, but he aint going out with her. He said they hadn't spoken in weeks. He said when he phones me, he'll say his name is Anthony just in case Janay answers the phone. My man has got it all figured out. Idiot. Johnathon's a joker, nothing can gwarn. He's meant to be with Alisha, so I don't know why he's trying it on with me. He kept saying "Alisha doesn't have to know." I aint sharing no man.

I'm sleeping at Gaynor's, mom's performing at a carnival tomorrow. Anytime I come here Gaynor treats me like a little kid, I love it. She makes me a hot drink and brings me pure sweets and stuff while I chill in bed, then me and her sit and chat. She always buys me rainbow drops, I aint got the heart to tell her that they taste so stale, you'd think they were outta date. But I love that she takes the time to listen and doesn't judge me. She'd be a great Agony Aunt.

Chana is at Sonia's and Janay's at Alisha's. I could have stayed home, but Gaynor said she wanted to talk to me and see how I was. I did wonder if there was any point staying at Gaynor's when she just lives next door! Gaynor was asking me how I feel about Nina and dad moving away, I said I hadn't really thought about it, she told me I should check in with my feelings and not to worry about feeling upset.

She was asking me about how I'm getting on at school and was anyone checking up on my progress, I said no one was really asking. She seemed really interested in what subjects I like, which are Geography and Food Tech. She said that if I wanted her to come to the next Parents Evening she would come with me. I rate her man. Before I went to sleep she was telling me all about where she lived in Yorkshire, it sounded dry, she said it was a historic county and that it's known for its Roman and Viking castles. She said it had two national parks. She's like a historian, she knows all about that place. It was nice to see her so interested in her hometown though still.

I looked dark today, I had blue stretch jeans on with a fitted top. Johnathon was saying that my jeans were 'airtight' and that my figure was dazzling his eyes! They were saying my jeans were more like leggings!

Johnathon stop watching me and start watching your actual gyal, Alisha. DICKHEAD.

Was meant to go with Dad but he had an urgent business meeting that he had to go to.

17th August 1997
I've come on today, my reds normally last for 4 days, that means I'll be on till at least Thursday. KISS MY TEETH.

Jade's in love with Bryson ha!! Bryson went with her to meet her cousins and her nan you know, (arl a meet de family) Do you think I could EVER ask Trayvon, or Elijah to come to my nans. HA! YUH MUST BE MAD.

Been feeling pissed off today. Sometimes I feel like runnin' away. I'm always getting in trouble or doing something wrong. I can't seem to please anyone really. Might speak to Gaynor about how I'm feeling, I don't really know how I'm feeling, I feel weird, just off, and low within myself.

Bryson tried to teef a Rolex from Diamond Directors. Leng came to our house looking for suspects. How's he gonna come from outta town and start that kinda bullshit?

Anyway, Imani signing off.

Oh, I've looked at the spelling of my name.... 'man' is in the middle of the 'I'. How weird is that 'cause men are always in the middle of my life, pissin' me off or annoying me. The two 'I's are separated from each other, kinda like how I feel, divided. If you say my name aloud 'Imani' it sounds similar to when you say, 'I'm angry'. Go on, try it: Say "I'm angry" then say "Imani," don't they sound the same? I guess I am angry anyway, so it does suit me. I wonder if there was any thought that went into my name or was it just something that was in fashion at the time? I wonder if my mom had high hopes for me when she chose that name, now look at me. Maybe it was a common name that everyone was choosing for their kids. Nothing special about it or me. They should have called me Camilla, the 'Ca' sounds harsh and angry. The 'Milla' sounds like killa. (I aint no killa, but I feel like killing a couple people at times) Camilla Evans would've sounded so fuked up, am I fuked up?

Imani go to your bed, it's not that deep. It's just a name.

Nah actually, the more I think about it, Chana sounds like a French wine, something nice. You know like, something proper classy.

Janay sounds French too, ok so all our names sound a bit French actually. There aint nothing French about us apart from the fact that we nyam couple baguettes on a weekend, the cheap no frills ones from Kwik Save! But even Janay's name sounds happy and positive, it reminds me of the word January which reminds me of new starts, new beginnings.

Whereas Imani is definitely the shittest name out of all three.

Actually, Nyah's aunt said my name meant faith and peace so maybe I'm not a mess. But that was the African meaning -I aint claiming nooooooo links to Africa!

I'm going to my bed.

18th August 1997

Today's been OK. I went to town to get Chana an inner tube for her bike. My dad got her a bike because her dad is wukless and she'd been asking mom for one for ages, but mom said she would have to wait a few more months till she saved up enough. When I mentioned it to my dad, he was like "why's Winston so wukless, me a guh buy har a bike even if a nuh my pikni'." And he went and got her a bike. The bikes nice still, she rides it everywhere. It's a grey and blue Carrera Luna Mountain Bike. It's got 21 gears, some proper tings. You should've seen Chana's face when she got it, she was buzzin'. Mom wasn't impressed though 'cause it made it look like she couldn't afford it, when in actual fact she was gonna get it the following month. Either way, Chana was happy, that's the main thing.

My hair needs washing, it's so dirty. That's a long ting man.

I can't believe what happened on Thursday, ME, AND ELIJAH. If Shola finds out, listen, my life won't be worth living. Monique was telling me that she's heard he IS with Shola properly and it aint no dibby-dibby relationship like what he's made it out to be.

Johnathon came down yesterday we were all at Charlton Park. He bought some drinks from the shop I got mash up and I lipsed him. I don't even know how that happened. SHIT.

LATER

19th August 1997
I went to town after school, I had on a white hipster skirt with a silver buckle and a blue fluffy top. My outfit looked dark.

I phoned Monique, she was telling me how she's bought Mary J' Blige's tune 'Everything,' and another bucket hat to go with her collection, I think she's bought a Helly Hansen one this time. Dwayne kept asking if I'm seeing, checkin, doing a ting, or anything with Dejuan. I said no, he's a BASTARD-I AINT interested I him.

I went shopping with mom today, just us two, I can't believe it. It was kinda weird because we didn't have that much to talk about.

I still can't believe I've done a ting with Elijah.

Oh yeahh, when I saw Mr Gold Teet in town, he was saying how he aint got time for Monique anymore and how she thinks she's too nice. He's the one that thinks he's nice, why's he still going on 'bout her! Monique loawed him agessss ago. He's the one still mentioning her name. He was telling me how he tried to get her beks at Shouters Night Club the other night by sitting near her but talking to me. I had no idea that men were this sly, imagine he was doing all that on purpose. Mr Gold Teet did look nice though, there's NO denying he's kriss. He said we probably won't see him for ages now because he's setting up a business with his cousins outta town.

I washed my hair today.

20th August 1997
Today I went Youth Club. Louise slept here.

Dwayne was asking me to do a ting with him. He's a joker, who just begs? (none of dat, he's hughly) he's with Natalie and furthermore Lashelle loves him off, and he aint my type.

21st August 1997
I lipsed Bryson yesterday. I know I shouldn't have, but it just kinda happened. He's kriss. We were talking and one thing just led to another. He kept saying I had a nice figure. He can't believe I'm 14. I lipsed him nuff times.

I feel bad for lipsing Bryson true he's done a ting with Jade, plus I think he tried it with Monique. When Monique asked me if she should do a ting with him, I said no because he'd done a ting with Jade. Now look what I've gone and done. Some matey business. Fukin hell. I never knew that I'd end up liking him though. So, it's not like I told her not to do a ting with him 'cause I liked him. I genuinely didn't think she should've, he'd already banged Jade so I weren't gonna tell Monique to go there too. When and if I tell Monique, she might think I'm fukry. I know what I did was wrong. Bryson kept asking if I was gonna tell anyone about what we had done (lipsed, I mean it's hardly anything to chat, chill!!)

If Monique finds out, we'll probably end up falling out, SHIT. This is fuked up man. I don't wanna lose my best friend.

I'm gonna have to speak to Gaynor about this Bryson situation, she'll know what I should do.

Janay got her results today she got six A's, three B's, one C, that's quite good. The house phone is on incoming calls only. AGAIN.

22 August 1997
Bryson went back home today. I lipsed him before he went. Lashelle asked me if I did a ting with Bryson. Is she his keeper? It's your half-brother, not your man. Either way, I denied it all the way. Get out my business.

Janay got a new Sony Mars Bar mobile for passing her exams, the phones dark. Dad came up, he was in a brand-new car, shiny alloys, tinted windows, and leathers, yooooo it looks heavy. He took out his personalised Parker pen and wrote me a cheque for £100 to put in my bank. I gave him my passport photo so hopefully I'll be going to Jamaica soon.

Me, Janay, and Chana have all got different dads. Them pair don't see their dad's that often, its fuked up really. I might share some of my money with them. Chana's dad Winston works away (apparently), and Janay's dad got locked up years ago. I don't know what he did, but he's got a serious bird.

Popped in on Gaynor today and told her 'bout Bryson, I explained that Jade had done a ting with him and then Monique asked me if she should do a ting with him, I told her not to because he'd already been with Jade. Monique agreed not to do anything with him, then I've only gone and found myself doing the exact same thing I told Monique **not to do**. Gaynor understood, she said I shouldn't worry and that it wasn't intentional or malicious, she did say that I should have a break from these boys! Maybe she's right.

23rd August 1997

I was speaking to Dwayne today and he was telling me how he aint checkin' Natalie, he's such a liar, I don't believe him. He said he's heard she's been bangin nex' man and he don't wanna know her anymore.

I heard that Caleb's supposed to be lock up. That would explain why we aint seen him for the last 3 months.

24th August 1997

Monique's heard what them lot have been saying about her being a skettel. I didn't tell her, someone else did. She's screwin' man. I don't blame her to be fair.
LATA ON.

25th August 1997

Today was almost as boring as yesterday. I went to bed at 6.30am.

I heard that Caleb's been sentenced. Trayvon's gonna be pissed, they're like brothers. He's got 2 years, but he's only doing 12 months, lucky rarse.

Chana's got a new Adidas tracksuit today. Mom doesn't let her wear anything except name brand. Fila, Nike, Ellesse, Michigan, Tommy Hilfiger that's literally all she wears.

I've taped some tunes off the radio today, Taurus Riley, Freddie McGregor and Beres; I love some of these old-time tunes.

Louise phoned me today, she hogs the conversation and never lets me get in a word, it does my head in.

26th August 1997

I've been up from 6am. I had to get Chana ready because she was going out with her dad. He aint been and seen her for ages, so I needed to make sure she looked good, really its him that should be making the effort. DICKHEAD. Janay had already plaited up her hair. Chana's dads name is Winston; I don't think my mom likes him true he doesn't come and see Chana that often. He works away in the Army, that's his excuse for not seeing her as often. I reckon he chats shit, we wouldn't know when he's away or not. Kids need their dad's man, these fukers think its ok to pass through as and when they want, some joke ting. Mom said his favourite phrases is 'I promise I'll see Chana soon'.

I phoned Monique today she said that she went shopping and that she's bought the same stretch jeans as me. Why's she piratin' me, there's that many coloured stretch jeans she could have, fukin 'ell man? She's got bare money; she could have any jeans that she wanted, why's she on my tings. Stick to your bucket hats and stop copying me man. Now I know how dad feels about his friend Paul copying the car that he's got.

I went to town to put that cheque in from my dad.

27th Aug 1997

I went to Youth Club. Dwayne was asking for a bang, what's wrong with him. I swear he's meant to be with Natalie. Too many man who have already got gyal are asking me to link them:

- Johnathon is with Alisha
- Bryson is with Jade
- Elijah is with Shola,
- Dwayne is with Natalie,

I think there's a couple more, but I can't even think of them all. Tramps.

28th August 1997

Yesterday Dwayne was telling me that he's an old darg (he was proud of it; he was boasting 'bout bangin' nuff gyal) how can anyone be proud of being an old' darg. He was saying I should link him true he's got a year's more experience than Dejuan. Joker. Today I heard that Bryson's banged Jade.

I aint going Jamaica, not sure why but dad said it's not happening anymore. I wonder if him and Nina are gonna split up. Seems strange that it's just cancelled like that. It can't be the expense 'cause they've both got money. Maybe she was complaining about not having enough space in the suitcases for all her Cosmopolitan magazines, ha! Or maybe they've had an argument about the separate room situation. I wonder if she's finally speaking up instead of being a doormat. Maybe she spoke up about how she was feeling, and dad just shut her down and said he aint going. I know dad probably wouldn't have given her too much air play.
Lashelle knows I've done a ting with her half-brother Bryson. For Fuk Sake.

29th August 1997

Today was good. The sound system was out at Midpoint Youth Club and everyone was there, pure music was playing, it was good man. Today my hair looked good, so did my outfit. I had on black battie riders and a white vest top.

I need to take £10 out my bank. I need some butterfly clips and some more camera film.

I need to get my bra size measured, I'll go to Contessa soon, it's this really nice underwear shop, it's a bit expensive, but the stuff is proper man.

30th August 1997

Bryson came down today. Me and Janay were telling him what Jade used to be like back in the day. She used to be a real tramp, she never used to fix up. When we used to go to her house her room was nasty, duti-e pants on the floor, yo it was a disgrace. She used to keep plates and cups in her room for weeks suh till all the mildew had formed, yo she was narsty. Its only since she's been staying with us and Janay's shown her to fix up that she's carrying herself a bit better. Janay's had to show her how to cook, clean and wash plates, bare stuff.

I asked Bryson if he liked me, he said yeahh of course! I think he's just sayin' that to make me feel sweet.

Oh yeah, Imogen's mom got a 9-month contract in Greece, she works as a Nanny, so they're moving there for a while, I'm so jealous. Imogen aint impressed though, she doesn't wanna go! Well, the further away she is the better it is for me she can keep her eyes off people's man.

I'm 's'ing.

31st August 1997

Princess Diana died today. It's been all over the news and everything. Apparently, it happened in the early hours, she died in hospital from a car accident in a road tunnel in Paris. MADNESS.

Last night, well this morning me and Bryson were on the phone till 7am, he told me that he'd liked me for ages and he just never knew how to tell me. Janay's gone Shouters. I aint been nowhere today, stayed in my yard. I was thinking I could bups:, Bryson and Johnathon. Nah gyal like me can't be fukry and juggle so many man. My life is messed up at the moment.
Banged Elijah
Lipsed Johnathon
Lipsed Bryson.

1st September 1997

Today's been sooo shit. I went to town to look for some school shoes. Jordan was in town, I haven't seen him since he got kicked out of school for the weed. He was saying his moms looking to move outta town 'cause she wants better for him. Today this little 13-year-old bwoy asked me if I wanted piece, I can't even remember his name, is he stupid?? gweh with your little 13-year-old self, 'bout do I want piece. What a joker. I just started laughing at him.

2nd September 1997

Today Bryson read most of my diary. I CANNOT BELIVE IT. FUK ME MAN, HE READ EVERYTHING. He said that he's not the only one that's read my diary and that 5 people have read it before him, 5 people, who the fuk are these 5 people? Bryson went back home for good today, he only came down for the 6 weeks holiday. I lipsed him before he went (obviously).

I'm thinking about the fact that Bryson has read my diary and other people. When he was reading it, I was trying to grab it off him, but I couldn't reach, all the pages started to fall out as well. I could have cried. He did say that he felt bad for invading my privacy. Fuk off, that was after you read ALL my business, fuk you. He got beks about what I wrote about me thinking of bupsing him, well that will teach you to read my things. The look in his eyes at the thought of me saying I would bups him was sad, I felt bad for writing that.

3rd September 1997

Louise was meant to come up after she got her hair done, but she never. Janay washed my hair for me today, of course she had to go on about how I should take more care of it. Just wash it and shallap. I swear she thinks she's a hairdresser! You work in a kids ball pit not Wavez and Stylez.

When we were out earlier today this man was trying to chat to Lashelle, he was in a white car. Lashelle told him she was 14 and my man was still trying to lyrics her. Tramp, my man looked at least 25 years old. CRAZY.

4th September 1997

Oh yeahh, the reason Louise didn't come up yesterday was because her brother, the one who hallucinates was found hanging from the light fitting, he tried to hang himself you know. Good job someone found him, that could've been a madness.

Mom gave me £50; I bought some loafers, they're nice they were £30, a pinafore dress £15 and a shirt that was £4, uniforms sorted now. I just need stationery for school, oh and a relaxer kit, hair needs to look fly for when I go back, you get me.

Johnathon phoned today and said he's finished with Alisha and how he wants me. Fuk me, this is becoming too much PRESSURE. What's he on about?? I didn't tell him to dun with her for me you know. I aint trying to be his gyal, one lips and now he's trying to get with me?

5th September 1997
Went to town, got my stationery and the relaxer kit. We saw Elijah, and his friends. Elijah phoned me-and we were arguing. (can't be bothered to explain) but mainly he said:

- I'm inconsiderate
- I don't appreciate shit
- I think I'm too nice
- I think only of myself
- He doesn't hate me, he gone past that stage

Bastard. He doesn't even know me like that. I'm too mad right now.

6th September 1997
Today was Princess Diana's funeral. It's been all over the news. It's so sad man. The news have shown the whole thing from Westminster Abbey to St James's Palace.

I've heard that Johnathon's meant to be dealing with one girl called Letisha. What on earth? He's a tramp. She wears this piercing, like a pig ring. She looks like an actual pig; you know them things they wear around their nose. She thinks it looks good; it looks dumb. What does she favour in hers?

I phoned Monique and told her about yesterday with Elijah, she could not believe it. I phoned Elijah, he came on the phone acting all nice and everything, he didn't mention how wrenk he was to me yesterday. He was asking if me and Lashelle would meet him outside Horizon Flats at 00.30am. We carried on talking and he kept asking if we were gonna go, I said no. Two two's he said, "open your front door." I said "what you on about?" He said "I'm outside." I said "no you aint." He said "open the door," so I went outside and spoke to him, I can't believe he was outside. Who just turns up? It was 00.50am, he was chattin' shit. I went back inside.

He kept ringing the house phone all till 3.30am. I put the phone down on him. He was being too wrenk. He was getting mad. Then he said he's gonna knife me up in my neck and if I see him on street I better run, 'cause NO-ONE puts the phone down on him and how I must be out of my mind. When I asked him to calm down and that I wanted to go to my bed, he said "yeahh your gonna have a warm night." Was he gonna burn down the house? He's a mad man. He said I was too cheeky and no GYAL talks to him the way that I do, and that I must think he's a dickhead.

8th September 1997
Went to Shouters. Elijah was there; he was staring at me all night. He was chattin' me blatantly to his friends like I couldn't hear him. He was pointing at me while he was talking, so it was obvious. PRICK.

Me and Monique relaxed our hair today, mine looks dark. Monique's ends weren't taking, they were all frizzy; I used the Dark and Lovely kit, but she used the Pink Lotion kit, maybe that's why hers came out dry. We got Alisha to cut the ends off.

9th September 1997

Today I went with Lashelle to town before school so that she could get her school blazer. She had to go Blazers Direct, they're one of the cheapest places to go. So glad that I didn't have to look in there for mine, thank God. Their blazers look and feel cheap man. I got mine from Marks & Spencer.

Considering it was the first day back, school was good today. It's probably the only time I'll ever say that! But I feel more independent, probably because I'm a homework monitor. (Nooo Imani, that's not something to be biggin' yourself up about! But I do like the responsibility).

Lashelle was pissin me off today, she was dissin me 'cause I had cold sores on my lips. I suffer with them bad man. They did look horrible though, not gonna lie. She does my head in, by the looks of our timetable I won't be spending that much time with her anyway thank goodness. She's got Music every day, the only lessons we have together are Science and R.E.

10th September 1997

School was a joke. I like being in year 10, I'm in top set for English, yeahh. Yesterday Lashelle was dissin me 'bout my cold sores and guess what, the gyal has come to school with a bag of them on her mouth. Fukin brute, that'll teach her to keep her mouth shut. Me and Louise were taking the piss out of her today.

Lashelle kept picking on Kim today saying that she thinks she's black true she busses cornrows (when did wearing cornrows in your hair make you think you're black?) I felt bad for not sticking up for Kim a bit more. But after all the mix up she causes it kinda served her right. I always stick up for her and she don't appreciate it. She doesn't get Janay to do her hair anymore she's been goin' to Wavez and Stylez in town instead.

Oh, there's a rumour going around that one girl that goes to Greenfields school is a hood sucker, the tramp.

11th September 1997

Went to town, this boy called Corey was chattin' me up, he gave me his number. He asked me to meet him in town on Saturday at 3pm, I said I'll see. I was telling Janay, she said she knows who he is and that he aint good looking at all. Monique said that he weren't all that either! Then this other boy came up to me, he said his name was Kerr, he was trying to chat to me too. Too much manz, too bloodclart much! There's only a few that are nice looking. My horoscope was right about today being 'my loved up day'.

Letisha and a few of her friends came to our school runnin' up their gums about that Alisha and Johnathon business. Alisha was bummy. Johnathon's been seeing Alisha and Letisha and now they're arguing, no surprise that no one's cussin Johnathon. Some joke ting. Glad no-one knows that he's been tryin' to chat to me. I phoned Monique today and gave her the lingwa, I told her 'bout the ruckus with them lot coming down to the school. Janay told me that Alisha isn't interested in Johnathon now she knows about Letisha.

12th September 1997
Johnathon the old darg was *still* asking me to be his gyal. After all the fukry he caused between Alisha and Letisha he can forget that. He was trying to sweet me up by saying he would pay me into the Puff Daddy Concert. Now that is tempting! He's got money though; I should make him spend it on me actually. HA.

Met this boy in town called Jaxon, we exchanged numbers, he's got a rough kinda look to him, but I actually like it. His hair is quite bushy, and he's got quite a bit of facial hair, he looks ok. He's mixed race, or he could be black but light skin, I'm not sure.

13th September 1997
I went to town today; everyone was up there. I had on a nice skirt and a nice top. Them manz were saying it should be a crime to show off as much leg as I was, jokers.

All today when I was talking to people I kept calling them Dejuan, how mad is that. Apparently when you keep calling someone's name it means they're thinking of you, well he should be thinking about me especially if he's stuck with that dry head gyal!

14th September 1997
Janay and Alisha have gone to Shouters, Alisha's sleeping here. Jaxon phoned me today, he was saying I should worship the ground he walks on because he's good looking.

What kinda man bigs up their own looks? Fool. He thinks I'm 15/16 and that I go to college!

Monique stayed in, she said she had homework to do, but I bet Marcia's saying she can't come out, she's strict when she's ready, trust me. Monique was telling me that her mom might be going on TV to talk about the work she does for women's rights. Gwarn Marcia.

Oh yeah, today Alisha asked me if Johnathon had ever asked me to do a ting with him. How awkward. Why's she asking me that? I obviously said no. But really I should have said yeah and made her know what a little tramp her man is. Why the hell I defended him is beyond me. Anyway, school a marnin' so I'm essing.

15th September 1997

I might join the Gospel choir at school. Noooooooooo Imani, don't big up the Gospel group! But nah seriously, my voice is dark still. Hear this anyway, Nyah told me that she's heard that Lashelles wrote a letter to Bryson and how in the letter she's calling me a slag. Okayyyyyyyyyyyy. It's like that then yeah.

Me and Nyah went to Monique's we were there from 6-9pm, just ketchin some joke. When I got back Janay said that Jaxon had phoned me. Can't believe I missed his call.

My science lesson was so dry today, fuk me where do they get these teachers from, they're shit. Everyone chats in the lesson and we never learn fuk all. The teacher is a knob.

Everyone was dissin Lashelles blazer today, it was so funny. Them lot asked her where she got it from and she said Woodberry, this time it from Blazers Direct, I know 'cause I went with her to buy it. There's no way she could tell them it was from there, she'd get run.

16th September 1997

I'm doing really well at school in most areas, but today school was so frustrating. Nyah and Lashelle aint talking again, all over that letter business, I asked Lashelle if she called me a slag and she's denying it, it's just some mix up. I was left in the middle of the argument.

It's hard because I'm talking to both of them, so I didn't know who to hang around with at dinner time. I didn't want anyone to think I was taking sides.

Anyway, Louise was telling me that Brianna (the one that's meant to have lipsed Dejuan when I was checking him, who is also now meant to be with him) wants to talk to me, talk to me 'bout what? I told Louise to tell her that I aint got nothing to talk to her about, she's a little skettel, I think she did lips him when I was with him because it's funny now that they're together. Bright and wrenk, 'bout she wants to talk to me. GWEH

Jaxon phoned me today, he said that he really wants to see me. I might go see him on Saturday to shut him up. I asked Jaxon if he liked Monique, he said no, you mad. He said she's got a big head as in literally. Hold on, not that she's big headed, but that she's actually got a big head; as in the size of it. He aint got no manners. He was being dead serious!

17ᵗʰ September 1997
P.E was ok today, we did aerobics. I completed my social science work. I've finally managed to curl a decent fringe; it looks OK to be fair. I'm up to date with all my homework and classwork. I'm tired, gyal like me is going to get some beauty sleep.
Janay's sending off for her provisional today, I wish I was older so that I could learn to drive. Get me out of this fukin house that's what I'd do first.

18ᵗʰ September 1997
We saw Trayvon today after school and he was saying how he aint a playah no more and how he's got a flat now. It's on the 9th floor, door number 11, not far from where I live. He gave me his new mobile number and his house number too. I think he's still checking L'Neisha though, I aint heard any different. If he aint a playah anymore, whys he giving me his number, knowing full well he's still with her. DICKHEAD.

Me and Brianna are talking now, she stopped me in the corridor at school and begged me to hear her out. I just said ok then, couldn't be bothered to keep up the old argument.

I've finally posted my letter to Bryson.

Summer romance with Bryson has done. KISS MY TEETH.

19ᵗʰ September 1997
Jaxon phoned me about three times today he was telling me how he's not a typical outta town man and how he aint no rapist. Who says I'm not a rapist when they're trying to

chat up gyal? I know there's loads of stories going round about outta town man raping gyal etc, but by saying you aint a rapist just makes me think you're weird. I can see why he has said it though, 'cause nuff gyal are going outta town and getting into madness with the manz up there, they're calling it rape. I don't think its rape, as in real actual RAPE, but more like, when man are trying it and you're just playing around kinda vibes. Fuk knows, either way I aint trying to be in any of that bullshit. He wants me to link him tomorrow, he gave me his address 999 Norset Tower, Ladyfield.

He told me it was near the Florence Pub. I should know by the door number that he's danger and the fact that he lives in **Lady**field should tell me he's a gyalist. He is kriss though, Jheeze.

He was saying that I was lucky to even be asked to come to his house, 'cause nuff gyal are begging him to give them his address. Oh please. I don't mind going outta town to see him, but I aint going to his flat, I'll tell him when he calls me tomorrow. (He aint gonna like the sound of that though) to be honest, I can't see me even being bothered to go tomorrow.

20th September 1997

It's Janay's birthday today, she'll probably be going out raving somewhere. I bought her some Ellesse trainers from the money that dad gave me that was in my bank, hope she likes them. Today I was supposed to meet Jaxon, but I couldn't be bothered, I went to town instead. Who do I see in town? Jaxon. So, if I had gone to see him, he wouldn't have been there anyway, could you imagine me boppin all that way and my man aint even there. He barely spoke to me when he saw me, he just said he'd call me tomorrow. Why the hell was he blanking me? This time the man was on my line yesterday. TWAT.

We saw Letisha in town, she was runnin' up her mouth with one gyal, the girl just stood there and took it. Letisha was saying that she's with Johnathon and if the girl doesn't stop telling people that *she's with him*, she'll box her down. You think I'd make any gyal come and try chat to me like some idiot. I don't know who she thinks she is. Fuk Letisha anyway, she's a slag, talking of slags, I saw Kim today. I was talking to her for a bit. Things aint the same between me and her these days, so much has happened, I'm still cool with her, we're just not as tight as we used to be. She looked good though, she had on a dark DKNY tracksuit and some new trainers. She tried to fren me up askin' if I wanted anything from McDonalds, I told her I was good. Don't want nuen from that gyal.

Jaxon aint phoned me today.

I saw Natalie today, I asked if she was still with Dwayne and she said, "yeah me and him will never done." If she only knew how much the man is on *my* line.

I read something that said, men think about sex every 6 seconds. Imagine that! Tramps!

Janay's sleeping at her friend's house and moms gone to perform at another show, I think it's a club called 'Sasha's'. Chana's staying with Sonia. I'm home alone again. I don't mind though. I like when the house is quiet and I can just be here in peace. Well, sometimes its lonely, but I like being on my own. No one really gets me anyway.

21st September 1997

To Floyd, yesterday I was thinking of you. I miss you. I always think about you. It's hard to believe that you're gone. I hope you can see how much I cared about you. We are going to visit your gravestone again soon. I promise. You were so special and so good looking, those hazel eyes, or were they contacts!! Either way, they really suited you. Rest in Peace. Always xxx

Why did you leave?

Why did you go?

Is there a reason, nobody knows?

You're here today, gone tomorrow,

Leaving family and friends in tears and sorrow

How we wish you'd lived to see another day

But now you've gone, you've flown away

The one thing we loved

Were your deep hazel eyes

When we remember you

We start to cry

I hope one day, we'll meet again

I'll never forget you, Floyd our friend

Xxxxx

Jaxon phoned me today. Man wants to talk now but couldn't chat in town.

I got £5 from Gaynor for doing her ironing, when I was there I was telling her about Jaxon, she said "he sounds like a loser, don't waste your time Imani." She's a joker you know, I love our little convo's. I asked how she's getting on with the book, she said she's almost finished. She had to stop reading it for a while because she was waiting on some new glasses and the opticians were taking the piss to get them sorted for her.

22nd September 1997

Nyah and Lashelle are kinda talking a bit more now. At dinnertime I phoned Trayvon, he was giving me some joke. I should be buying my Puff Daddy ticket tomorrow, none of these idiots have bought me one. Good job I don't rely on them for anything. My horoscope was right, 'listen to my heart' and get shit done myself.

Been in my yard all day working on this coursework. Mom got us McDonald's for dinner. Janay's bought Missy Elliott's new tune 'The Rain' and Puff Daddy and SWV's new tune 'Someone'. The two tunes are dark. Monique wants to hurry up and get her ticket. THIS is one concert that I AM NOT MISSING out on. Plus, I don't wanna be boppin' to the concert with Jade. (yes, she is coming, my gyal is too eggs-up)

23rd September 1997

Jade finally went back to her house today; her mom's finished the nursing course. THANK GOD. Dwayne phoned me today begging for a bang, I told him to fuk off, so he put the phone down. DICKHEAD. He's still denying that he's with Natalie, what's that about? I saw her a few days ago and she's definitely saying she's with him. I've no time to be entertaining Dwayne and his nonsense.

Went to town got my ticket for Puff Daddy but there's a rumour going around that its cancelled. I hope it aint, I've been looking forward to this from when. In town Umpa Lumpa Ebony was outside Pearly Whites begging everyone to get her a ticket, most people were just walking past her. Then I saw her cussin' one gyal and searching her pockets, she took the girls pager, and about twenty pound off her. She's outta order man. The girl stood there; she couldn't do anything. No one even bothered to help. Ebony would've just boxed them down anyway. Queen Cartel Squad were in town, they were getting their tickets for the concert too.

24th September 1997

I did hockey afterschool, I didn't mind it. It's the one sport that I'm ok at. Lashelles P.E top was jack up; everyone was laughing. It was so small, I don't know where she got it from, but it was tiny. Oh, it's true that the Puff Daddy Concert has been cancelled, can't believe it man. But I heard it's going to be put back on the 14th February next year. And we all know that day would be dark.

25th September 1997

Nyah was pissin' me off and I had a major headache as well. Hardly anyone was at school today, everyone was off skiving. I might join the skiving crew, school's starting to do my head in.

I went to Youth Club and then to Monique's for a bit.

26th September 1997

Instead of going to school, all the black people were invited to Central Station Youth Club to talk about the types of things we want to see in the area that would help us achieve and succeed. Loads of people from different schools were there, it was joke, we gave them loads of suggestions. They better put them into action, these people love to ask your opinion, but they don't do shit. It's about time they did something for us. We asked for black food to go on the school menus regularly, not to just learn about black history once a year but for it to be part of our everyday lessons, we asked if we could have more black teachers at school so we've got people who look like us and that we can relate to, we asked if we can have black hairdressers come into school and talk to the girls 'cause our hair is the main reason why we skive swimming lessons, and we asked if we could have guests to come in to inspire us about how they started their businesses and stuff. Let's see what they come up with.

Saw dad today in his Tom Ford tracksuit, he's so extra! He had the roof down on his car, the sun wasn't even shining too tuff, he's just boasy!

Dwayne was asking Lashelle for a bang. I told Lashelle that he's always phoning and begging me for sex too, she said that Dwayne told her he's only messing about when he asks me. WHATEVER. I can assure you if I wanted him (which nobody does) I could have him.

Lashelle's sprained her wrist at school and now it's in plaster and bandaged up, everyone's saying she's been wanking too many man, that's why her wrist is mash up. People aint got no manners!

27th September 1997
Today dad bought me a CD and cassette player, its dark, it cost £250. I've wanted one for ages. I saw some cheaper ones, but dad was saying cheap things don't last and was asking why've I got a cheap mentality. You try living in a house with two sisters and think your brave enough to ask your single mom for a £250 cassette player-you must be mad.

We all went town after school, saw Jaxon and his crew. Jaxon looked tick. Him and his friends stole some Versace coats from this designer shop. They made a raise still.

28th September 1997

I saw Johnathon today, he kept asking if I wanted anything from the shop, the joker. He thinks that Wham bars and Push Pops are gonna make me wanna chat to him, what an idiot. He said he's got a day off work tomorrow and do I wanna go cinema! Cinema?...listen, I've got school to go to, bout cinema. I told him not to chat to me when he sees me. I'm not interested in him and his bullshit.

Janay and Alisha have gone Shouters Night Club. I've been chattin' on the phone and listening to music, my favourite three tunes at the moment are Destiny's Child 'no, no, no', EnVogue 'Don't let go' and KP and Envyi 'Shorty swing my way'. I love these tunes.

29th September 1997

Today my hair looked dark. (The front was gelled down; the middle was in a side beehive and the back was all out and curled). Homework's all done. Its only 10.20pm and the whole house are in bed, madness. I may as well go to mine too.

30th September 1997

Janay told me that there's a rumour going round that Johnathon's saying he's seeing me, I was like, what, is he mad? Seeing me? A couple lips's and man's feeling sweet and telling people we are seeing each other. Listen, he needs to loawe it. He can stay there with Letisha. I aint trying to get involved with them and their nonsense. She can keep him.

I told Janay to tell Alisha that I saw Letisha in town the other day, and how she was cussin' one girl saying how she's with Johnathon. We were all laughing, we feel sorry for them gyal. Jonathan will just carry on taking the piss out of them both. Alisha said she was glad she wasn't with him anymore. I'm glad he doesn't call my phone now either.

Lashelle's a knob she was trying to diss and say that most of the boys I've checked are ugly, this is coming from her, who can't even ketch man and is getting excited true Dwayne has paid her a bit of interest. FOOL.

1st October 1997
After school we went to Youth Club only to find that it was closed 'cause of a staff meeting, so we all came back to mine.

Lashelle keeps asking questions about me and Dejuan, there is no me and Dejuan, when I say this gyal is nosey.

Oh yeah, I heard that Jaxon and his crew got caught and sent to penn for that raise they did on the Versace coats in town, think they got about 4 years between them, madness.

2nd Oct 1997
Jade came up today. I don't hate her; I just think that she goes on immature and fool sometimes. Nyah was doing my head in during Maths today. Heard that Nathaniel's been excluded from school for that thing with Mrs Kumar too. Ha Brute.

3rd October 1997

Mom's birthday today. Sonia (mom's best friend) and Gaynor have come round.

I cooked them all a wicked meal, she likes lasagne's and jacket potatoes so that's what I made. Mom waxed it off, she really liked it and said it tasted almost as good as the ones she makes. Yeah! Gaynor winked at me as a sign of approval that she also liked my Lasagne. Yo don't watch my cooking, if I don't make it as a Nurse, I'd love to be a Chef.

I spoke to Kim's mom Kath about Nursing, she said the shifts were long and that you never got fixed hours, she said I shouldn't bother with nursing as a career. No-one seems to be encouraging me to do it. Only Gaynor routes for me. Gaynor even said she would help me get some work experience in a hospital. That'll be good.

Youth Club was ok. After Midpoint everyone went over to the park, chilling and chattin'. I'm sleeping at Monique's tomorrow, it should be joke.

4th October 1997

Us lot went town, all the Rising Star manz were there. Mom gave me £10 and I saw my dad and he gave me £50 too.

Dad said "Imani nuh spend arf all de money, try put sometin' down fe a rainy day." I should save some and not spend it, I do try to but its hard man. Isn't saving for big people! He can't give me them kinda responsibilities when I'm just out here trying to live my life ha. Maybe one day.

When we were on the bus leaving town, we looked out the window and saw Ebony boxing up this girl cussin' her saying how she aint black and that if the girl wanted to wear cornrows and Fila shoes she had to pay Ebony. MADNESS. I'm glad we were on the bus. I wanted to help the girl; I hate when I see people going on like that.

5th October 1997

Alisha's sleeping here. Her and Janay are going to Shouters later. One of Janay's other friends has been kicked out of her mom's so our mom said she can stay with us. The whole house is ram out. Everyone's gone out now, I'm just here with Chana chilling. She's playing with her Tamagotchi so she aint bothering me!

6th October 1997

Today's been shit, my house phone has been cut off; it aint going back on till Wednesday. At school everyone went chip shop at dinner time, anyhow the teachers find out. But it's gonna be obvious that we weren't in school, all the black kids just went missing!

I went to town after school, I bought bare CD's; Janet Jackson, Jodeci, Mase, Foxy Brown, Mark Morrison and Blackstreet, CD collections looking fat. I saw Kim today at the school opening evening, she chats shit. She was saying how she's checking this 27- year- old man. Twenty rarse seven you know. I swear it's like she's looking for trouble. Gaynor came with me to the opening evening-I fully rate that.

7th October 1997

I stayed in all day, sorted my homework, and got that all up to date. I've stayed in my pjs all day. I've cleaned the house from top to bottom as well.

8th October 1997

Youth Club was shit. Ebony was there, we saw her teefing sweets from the tuck shop and putting it under her coat. I asked Monique if we should tell Patsy and Nigel the youth workers but she was like, nah we shouldn't 'cause if Ebony found out it was us; we'd be fuked.

9th October 1997

Homework's all done, everyone's chattin' Monique saying how she loves man too much and how she loves the attention.

At school we are making up a dance to MC Lyte 'Cold Rock a party', the routine is dark.

I've changed my bedroom round (again!) When I was sorting my room, I saw some tablets in Janay's drawer, they looked like ecstasy tablets. I remember the teachers giving us a lesson about the different types of drugs and what they look like, they're definitely ecstasy tablets. They were all different sizes and colours; they had a logo on them. I remember the teachers saying the logos had something to do with the labs they were made in. I aint gonna say anything though, I aint no informer.

I've been in all day, except when I went to the shop to get my ingredients for tomorrow's cooking lesson. Mr Singh's shop is like a warehouse, he sells EVERYTHING. Crisps and chocolates are next to the paper clips and hair bobbles, the cooking oil is on the next aisle next to a random tin opener. They sell everything in there. I had 10p change and was about to buy a 10p mix until I saw Mr Singhs hand go in the tub, I had to tell him to use the tongs. Fuk knows where his hands have been and he's trying to share out sweets for me, I can count to 10 yah know.

10th October 1997

My house phone's back on, finally. Dwayne was trying to lyrics Lashelle, (he's an old darg fe true) he just goes from one gyal to the next all the time. I'm glad that he's stopped bothering me, he can have Lashelle. Mom and Janay have gone to Ace-1 Radio's Birthday party. I'm at home watching Chana, she's in her room chilling, she's cool. She doesn't piss me off like everyone else does.

News is spreading that some paedo's are lurking round the area, one gyal from school was supposed to have got beaten and kidnapped by them. Everyone's talking 'bout it, some madness. Mr Hanson wants anyone with information to go and see him, what information does he think we have 'bout peados? He fukin looks like a peado if you ask me!

11th October 1997

Went to town, I bought Foxy Brown and Dru Hills tune 'Big Bad Momma' and I bought Changing Faces G.H.E.T.T.O.U.T, the tunes dark. I love my music. I saw Elijah in town, he apologised for the argument we had last month, he said he'd call me later. I aint seen him since the start of September at that party.

I aint done no homework today, can't be bothered.

13th October 1997

Can't even remember what I've been doing over the last few days.

Today Elijah came to mine from 7pm till 4am. He bought me some snacks from the shop (Hooch and a bottle of 20/20 to share with him). I actually enjoyed his company today. I asked him 'bout Shola AGAIN, he told me he's tried to get rid of her, but she keeps saying she'll run on a train line and kill herself if he finishes with her. So, he's gotta stay with her, I guess? I saw Gaynor at the shop today and she asked me if I'd do some more cleaning, I'll go there tomorrow.

Today mom asked me if I'm taking drugs, what's she on about? How random? Drugs you know! She needs to ask Janay, not me!

14th October 1997

Today, Elijah and all them manz came to mine. They were giving me pure joke. I went to Gaynor's today, she asked if I'd heard back from Kerry Cook, my pen pal. I said I hadn't heard anything back and that I hoped she was ok. Gaynor was saying how pleased she was about the way I conducted myself at the Open Evening at school the other day. Well, I try! When I was there ironing, she said she'd finished the book now and she's gonna write to her daughter Eileen. I'm so pleased, hopefully this will be the start of them sorting things out. I was telling Gaynor that my mom asked me if I was on drugs, she started laughing. I asked what she found funny; she said that sometimes I seem withdrawn and quiet so that might be why my mom asked if I was on drugs. I'd love these adults to come and live a week in my life, they'd be withdrawn too. Bout drugs. KISS MY TEETH.

15th October 1997

School was ok, I had a hockey tournament. Lashelle was complaining that people weren't marking their players, she acts like it's the Olympics!! Its fukin school! Lashelle told Monique how I was whining up myself in front of the manz at the party the other day and how she had to tell me to calm down, why's she lying? Honestly this gyal is a troublemaker.

16th October 1997

Today's been joke. I went to a party, everyone was there. One boy called Scary-B gave Louise his number. He's sooo good looking. He's tall, he's got his nose pierced and always wears his cap real low. Jheeze. Gwarn Louise!! Party got locked off at 10.30pm, some early times. Leng came and locked it off and said there had been complaints from the neighbours about weed being smoked. How do the neighbours know what people are smoking INSIDE the party? What kinda nonsense, they're prob old and got fuk all better to do.

Trayvon was at the party, it's the first time I've seen him in ages.

17th oct 1997

Went Youth Club for a bit today, it was ok. Oh yeah, Monique won £10 in her pack of crisps today. They put these little blue envelopes inside the packs, and you can win money or a free bag of crisps, she's lucky man.

18th October 1997

Went to the new cinema with them gyal, it looked wicked. We didn't end up watching anything because by the time the show would've finished, we would've missed our last bus home. I bought three more CD's today, Brownstones tune called 'kiss and tell', Busta Rhymes 'Put your hands where my eyes can see and Jodeci 'Cry for You'. My collection is building up.

17th October 1997

I got a call today; when I answered, it was Shola, she was asking me about Elijah. How did she get my number? She seemed pissed off. I said I didn't know what she was on about *(I mean, I don't want her to go kill herself do I)*. I need to get in contact with Elijah ASAP to tell him that she's called me. I wonder what he'll say? If he goes back and tells her that I've told him, then she'll know that we do speak.

5th Nov 1997

Today we went to a party at Youth Club. At the end of the night Elijah was beeping the car horn after me, I carried on walking, after the whole Shola thing yesterday I couldn't be bothered to chat to him. He drove onto the pavement to get my attention. I told him about Shola phoning me. He said that Shola wouldn't be calling me again. I asked why. He told me not to worry. Fuk me, I wonder if he's gonna hit her or something? When I asked him again, he just kept saying, "don't worry Imani, I'll sort it." I hope I haven't got her into any trouble. SHIT.

3rd December 1997

Went to school at 2nd lesson, no real reason why, I was just taking my time.

I phoned Trayvon, he's safe, he was telling me how he loves L'Neisha. I think he was actually being serious. He said she's the first gyal that he has ever loved. Fuk me. Thanks Trayvon. PUNK. Trayvon's the first person I ever banged, it hurt to hear him say that about L'Neisha still. She aint even been in the country a year and he's telling me he loves her; I've liked him since 95, KISS MY TEETH. He was saying how she's going back to Jamaica for Christmas and New Years and that she'd back down in Feb/March, like I give a fuk.

Louise said that Scary-B called her the other day and that she's seeing him properly, as in checkin him now.

6th December 1997
I met Elijah at 6:30pm outside 'Miss. P's' Caribbean Takeaway food shop. We went cinema and watched Aliens Resurrected. I didn't really want to go to be honest, but I didn't feel like I had a choice. He told me to stop being miserable and that loads of girls would wanna be in my place right now and that I'd better fix my face.
He paid me in, he came back here afterwards, we were ketchin joke.

7th December 1997
Today Elijah phoned, he said he was coming up. All now I aint seen him and its 10:35pm. I phoned Monique today; she was telling me how Ebony went to her school and was waiting at the gates and taxing everyone's money. Monique was saying how Ebony tried to search her, but when Monique told her who her cousins were, Ebony backed off.

8th December 1997

I've heard that Shola's breeding for Elijah, what the hell?? I should loawe him, after all he is gonna be a daddy now. I don't really fancy Shola in my face. I was gonna phone him and ask him what happened to coming to see me yesterday, but I thought fuk it.

That's it really.

9th December 1997

I went to town after school, every shop was playing Mariah Carey's fukin 'all I want for Christmas' tune, the song is rinsed. I bought my dad some Versace Black aftershave for Xmas. All the Queen Cartel Squad were in town too, smoking and drinking like they're dark. School was shit. It was hectic, and the teachers were pissing me off.

11th December 1997

Janay's taken Chana to Uncle Vincent's house; I think they're gonna chill there for the day, they've caught the train up there. Janay never asked me if I wanted to go and to be fair I wouldn't have anyway. I aint that close with the family like that, I can't be bothered. I like my space. Plus, Uncle Vincent makes it clear that he prefers them two; so mek them gwarn.

12th December 1997

I've been trying to phone Elijah since 10-11pm. His phones been off. He must think I've got time to keep going to the phone box. Youth Club was ok I suppose. Nyah was supposed to knock me, all now I aint seen her.

13ᵗʰ December 1997

Went town, couple people were up there. Monique and Lashelle were slightly pissin' me off. I saw Louise in town, she looked dark still, she was on her way to Scary-B's yard. I've been trying to phone Elijah all day but as usual his phone was off. I've just finished watching one film called 'Jackie Brown', it was dark still. It was about this woman who works as a flight attendant, she got caught smuggling money and had to choose between siding with the feds, informing on her handlers or keeping her mouth shut and risk going to penn. Dark film still.

This time next week I'll be getting ready to go on a shopping trip with dad and Nina, I think it's just for the day, to go clothes shopping and stuff. It should be good, my wardrobe needs some updating.

14ᵗʰ December 1997

I was sweeping Gaynor's front garden and I looked up only to see Elijah standing there. He appears out of nowhere! He's like a stalker sometimes. He said his phone has been messing about, whatever! I asked him if Shola was breeding for him and he said yeah and started to tell me how excited he was 'cause he's having twin girls. WHATTT? If he knows the sex of the babies, that must mean she's quite far gone, how's he just saying this to me all casually. Am I meant to be ok with this? We spoke for a bit, then he kissed me on my neck and said he'd call me later. I can't believe what happened, the man is actually gonna be a dad and acted like I asked him the FUKIN weather. I'm in shock.

Winston, Chana's dad dropped off some stuff for her and he bought her a play station. It's the first time I've thought about how much Chana does look like her dad, they've got the same skin complexion and the same chubby nose. He's really tall, I wonder if Chana will take that trait of his. I feel sorry for her if she does, 'cause tall gyal get dissed. He was saying to Chana, "You know I'm your dad, no-one else, make sure you never call anyone else dad." I overheard them talking. Janay must have heard too, she marched straight to him and cussed him out, she told him not to fill Chana's head with any bullshit and even though he is her dad he don't act like one, she went innnnn. She told him to move from the house and told Chana to get inside. He aint been around for Chana. Who was there for her when she lost her first tooth? Who was there for her at her first day of school? Who was there for her when she didn't' get the part of Mary at the school Nativity play and had to play the part of a Christmas tree (that was kinda' funny still!!) Me and Janay, that's who. Winston's wrenk though, he's got bigger things to worry 'bout than Chana calling someone else dad. Furthermore, mom's single anyway so what's he worrying about.

It's 3am and mom still aint come back, I think she's got two back- to- back shows tonight.

15th December 1997
Jade and Louise phoned me today, and someone else but I can't remember. My hair needs sorting badly.
Today's gone fast. I phoned Monique; she was being boring!! She can chat shit sometimes.

Nina phoned beggin' fren with me, she asked if I was 'devastated' about not going to Jamaica, I said I wasn't 'devastated', but I'd been looking forward to it. I asked her why we weren't going, she said that she heard dad was having an affair with Sonia behind her back, but she wasn't 100% sure so she called it off. I said **WHAT?** I asked her if she's asked dad, she said that she hadn't because she was scared he would cuss her. Is she a FOOL? So that's why I kept seeing dad's car near Sonia's house...bout his friend Paul's got the same car as him. Everyone just lies don't they. I feel confused, am I meant to tell dad what Nina has told me, am I meant to keep my mouth shut? Does she want me to tell him? Was she trying to trick me? Do I tell mom about her slag friend, why am I now involved in big peoples business?

I'm gonna ask Gaynor what she thinks I should do.
Anyway, Later on!

18th December 1997

Louise slept over; we watched Scream 2, we laughed most of the way through it. Louise was telling me how Scary-B is shit in bed. We were both laughing our heads off. Considering he's so good looking, you'd think he was a performer! Louise was telling me how she has to teach him everything!

19th December 1997

It was the last day of school and we could wear our own clothes. I wore a tight tennis kinda dress. It looked dark. We stopped for a disco after school, it was ok, we performed our MC Lyte dance. Everyone was dancing to Mark Morrison's tune, Return of the Mac, I love that tune still.

The teachers were trying to sell them cheap Panda drinks, but everyone had bought in their own cans of pop. Elijah picked me up from school, I wasn't expecting it and he never told me he was coming. How did he know I was staying at school till 5pm? He knows EVERYTHING. I wanted to walk with them lot, but he told me to get in the car and that I was being ungrateful. All the teachers were going mad because he was razzing up his engine and making a scene. Plus, he was blasting DMX out and singing 'Come on, uh, uh? What 'cha really want. D-M-X, uh, uh? Come on, Ryde or die. What's my name? DMX and I be the best'.

Honestly how embarrassing was that.

20th December 1997

I think I'm growing to fancy Elijah a lot. He came up twice today. No-one was here. When he said he was going; I kissed my teet. He asked what I was kissing my teeth for, I said nothing. (Janay was at work 5pm-12:45am, Chana was at Sonia's everything would've been kriss for him to stay longer)

Monique called me today saying how people are saying I'm a skettel 'cause I'm with Elijah, I put the phone down on her and told Elijah what she said. He said everyone loves calling his name and that I mustn't worry 'bout any of that bullshit. I told him that the Shola thing was outa order, he said that it wasn't anything serious and how he's been trying to finish with her for ages and now she's ended up pregnant, and what was he meant to do now, leave her? **ENDED UP PREGNANT. YOU MEAN YOU FUKED HER. SHE DIDN'T JUST END UP PREGNANT.** I told him that we should stop seeing each other, he started laughing and said, I don't get to decide when we finish. He was laughing, so I didn't take it seriously, he's a joker.

I relaxed my hair today, that kit stunk up the whole house and I've got pure scabs on my hair now but fuk it my hair looks bone straight; that's all that matters.

I'm not going to dad's for X-mas, I think him and Nina are gonna be beks, but I'd be bored. Nina's a Seven Day Adventist now so you can only imagine the nonsense that she's gonna try if I go up there, nah fuk that. All of a sudden, she's worshipping Jehovah? She jumps on every trend (not that I'm saying religion is a trend), but I swear anything that's in fashion, Nina's on it.

She buys designers just 'cause they're name brand, not because they *actually* look good, she buys Cosmopolitan magazines 'cause her manager reads them, she aint got a mind of her own, she's a dyam arse. She's just follow fashion. Maybe she buys so much stuff 'cause she's lonely. I don't know who sits down knowing or thinking their man, no I mean HUSBAND has cheated and doesn't open their mouth. She's crazy! Dad aint that scary surely, furthermore if he's in the wrong, he's in the wrong, simple.

22nd December 1997

Today; me, Janay and Chana went to town, every rarse shop was blasting out Cliff Richards dry ass Christmas songs, no one gives a fuk 'bout mistletoe and wine. It's not often that all three of us roll out together. Janay got us McDonald's, shock horror, she's normally really stingy. I bought some Fila shoes and a Timberland Coat. They're dark. The coat was £140. Later on, me and Nyah went to

Monique's. On the way back Nyah caught her bus and left me to walk. Two twos, someone was beeping their car horn at me, it was Elijah. I asked him to give me a lift home. He said, "do I look like a taxi service?" So, I carried on walking. He beeped the horn again, this time I jumped in. When I got home I said I'd phone him, but he mumbled something that sounded like "nah, I'll phone you." It's late now and I aint heard from him, so I'm going to my bed.

23rd December 1997
I saw Elijah in town, he came back to my house. He gives me joke. I made him chicken pie, then he asked for some of my tinned jam pudding (craven) he left here at 4:45am. He wants me to buy him some jewellery for Xmas. My moneys tight so I can't see that happening. Oh, and he asked me my full name today. I'm not sure what he wanted my second name for? Either way, I told him. Imani Rochelle Evans.

I popped in on Gaynor today, she was blasting out Maxi Priest from her stereo! I told her what Nina told me about Sonia and dads narstiness. Gaynor told me that Nina was out of order for tellin' me and that she shouldn't have. Gaynor said that I shouldn't say anything as Nina might not have all the facts and she's the one married to dad and she needs to address any issues, not me.

What would I do without Gaynor? Love this woman- not in a weird lemon way. Just you know, as a person.

24th December 1997
Today's Christmas Eve. Moms covered the whole house with Christmas decorations, it looks like a grotto. We've got a giant pink metallic foil star in the middle of the living

room too, every minute my hairs getting caught in it, why are they hung so low? Got drawing pins dropping from the ceiling every minute. Moms spray painted the windows with that fake snow too, fukin hell. I was gonna ask her if we could rent a film from Blockbusters but I'm not sure she'll want to, especially like how we have Cable now. Home Alone 3 was released the other day but no-one aint looking to watch that, 1 and 2 were shit enough!

We were all supposed to go to Kim's, but she told us that her mom and step-dad have found out that she was linkin' that man who was wayyy older than her, so she's grounded. Imagine them finding out she linked a big man. He's been locked up from the start of the year, I'm sure it was about February that he got sentenced. I wonder how they've only just found out. Nyah and Monique came up to mine instead, we were chilling ketchin' joke.

Elijah came up three times today. We've been play fighting; his hits are sometimes quite hard though. I need to toughen up anyway. I don't want it to get too physical. I've heard that he used to hit some of his exes. It's just play fighting I suppose, I've not got anything to worry about. Janay's gone Shouters Night Club it's 12:45am and I'm bored like shit.

25th December 1997

Christmas Day. People in my yard were opening presents at 8:10am. Gyal like me were tired, no way was I looking to go downstairs at them early times. I stayed in my bed. In the afternoon we went to my Uncle Vincent's house, he bought Janay and Chana some presents and said he'd buy me something for my birthday in January.

126

I thought that was stink and facety. Why would you buy for two nieces and not the other, who the fuk does that? Its ok though. After that I couldn't really be arsed to be honest. My uncle did dinner, I weren't that hungry, so I left most of it. He made a trifle which no one ate, they taste shit. He must have realised that no-one was eating the trifle because he went and took out a mint chocolate flavoured Viennetta from the freezer. He thinks he's posh. What's with him and mint? I remember for my birthday he bought me a mint flavoured cake. I had a few Snowballs and a Cherry B; they didn't taste great but it was alcohol so why not?

Chana's been drinking Shloer out of a wine glass, she gives me joke, I swear she really thinks she's drinking big peoples drink! My little sis, she's too funny. Uncle Vincent got her a Mr Slush Maker, so she's been forcing us to try her new flavour inventions!

Couldn't wait to go home-fuk this family.

26th December 1997

Today Elijah phoned me, he came up. We were ramping and he was hitting me and trying to suffocate me. He was only messing about though. It was more like play fighting to be honest, nothing serious. Me and Louise went to 'Miss P's' Caribbean Takeaway food shop, it was joke. I'm getting to really like Elijah but today and Wednesday he has been really annoying. He may think it's a joke, but it does actually hurt sometimes. Maybe that's how it started with Shola, but I was being wrenk to him so it's kina my own fault I guess. I'm sure it was just playful, there's nothing in it. He just likes to ramp and be farse.

27th December 1997
Today I went to town with Monique to see what the sales were saying. On our way there she said I bet we see Elijah. Then two two's we were in Our Price lookin' for some tunes to buy, who did we see. Elijah. I feel like he follows me or has got some kinda spy watching me, he's everywhere I go. Monique bought some Nike Air Max trainers and a FUBU puffer jacket with her X-mas money, and another bucket hat. I think it's a Mighty Ducks one, or is it Raiders? Can't remember.

We went to Shouters. When I was getting ready to go Elijah came up. He told me that I looked nice.

28th December 1997
Nina called me some early morning times. I asked why she was calling so early, she told me she'd just finished her yoga and that 6am starts were *'extremely beneficial for the brain and helped realign her chakras'*. Her what??? I didn't even bother to ask her. I thought Seven Day Adventists weren't meant to call anyone during the weekends, this woman's already breaking the rules. I knew she hadn't researched the ting properly. I aint looking to go and spend any time with her. She's beggin' fren' off me, listen, you're with my dad, focus on that. I aint trying to be your stepdaughter you know.

Today was a lazy day. Kim phoned me today, she was telling me that the reason she was grounded was 'cause Kath found the B-Day card that she was writing to that idiot in prison and that it said happy 26th B-day. She said Kath was going mad. I can only imagine Kath's face when she saw that. Your 15-year-old daughter going out with a 26-year-old, madness.

29th December 1997

Today me & Monique went with Elijah for a drive. He picked us up, it was ok being with them I suppose. He was giving me pure joke. When I got home, I stayed in for the rest of the night.

30th December 1997

Today, me Janay and Chana went to town. I bought my camera film in to be processed. Janay got us a McDonalds. No-One else was really in town. Elijah came up but didn't really stay longer than 10 minutes, then he came back up about 10:45pm. Him and his friends were all here till 12:45am. They were giving me joke. Elijah dragged me by my leg along the floor outside in the rain for a laugh. I was screwin'. He thought it was funny. I don't get why he does it and no-one says anything.

Hear tha lique, all that stuff Kim told us 'bout her mom finding out about that idiot in prison was a lie, what's wrong with this gyal. Kath phoned the house today asking if I knew who Kim was holding drugs for? I was like what are you on about. Kath said that she found ten big blocks of weed and pure Scottish money wrapped up in elastic bands under Kim's bed. FUKIN HELL KIM, what have you done? Kath thinks I know what's going on, but I haven't got a clue. I asked Kath if I could speak to Kim, but she said that Kim weren't taking any calls until she started to talk up. She said Kim's got 24 hours to talk up otherwise she's calling the feds. Kim's a compulsive liar, bloody hell, I don't know anyone who can lie like her.

I wonder if that's how she's been able to buss pure new stuff lately? That would explain the Scottish £50 note she had on her the other day, bwoy.

Anyway, Locking off.

1998

New Year's Day

1st Jan 1998

The house phone rang at 7pm, but by the time I got to it, it'd stopped. I pressed 1471 to see who had last called; it was Elijah, I rang him back, but his phone wasn't responding. I phoned Monique and we were talking 'bout Elijah. Two two's I heard my door knocking' it was him, it's like he's got a sixth sense. It's a bit creepy though. He never stayed long. He told me to phone him at 11pm. Between the time he left (10pm) and 11pm, gyal like me were tired. I phoned him and said I was going to my bed. He weren't impressed, he said he wanted to talk and that I was being lazy. Before he hung up he said he'd call me tomorrow before 3pm or 4pm. I can't remember which one. It's 11:30pm now and the whole family are cotchin'.

2nd Jan 1998

Elijah phoned me some early morning times, he asked me if I wanted to go to Woodberry Shopping Centre. Mom's gone out to rehearsals, Janay's working, and Chana's at Sonia's, so I told him to pick me up. We picked up Monique. It was a long ass journey to Woodberry Shopping Centre, the joke is by the time we got there, we were only stayed for 20 minutes. Elijah said the place bored him. I asked if we could stay a bit longer especially considering how long it took to get there, he started laughing and said, no gyal tells him what to do. I wasn't *telling him* what to do-it was just a simple question, like wooow chill out. On the way back, he was driving like a mad man. I asked him to drive properly and he said it was my fault that he was driving like that 'cause no gyal has ever questioned him and that I was facety for asking to stay longer and that's what's got him mad. Me and Monique were getting slightly bummy. He dropped us back to mine and then he went.

I went to the cinema with them lot. Elijah told me to call him when I got back. After the way Elijah was going on today, I didn't really wanna call him, but I didn't wanna get more headache by not trying his phone. When I did phone him, his phone was switched off. That's the best thing that's happened today.

Janay's gone to a nightclub and mom's gone out for the second time today.

3rd Jan 1998
Today I went to town with them lot. Chana was begging to come, all she kept saying was "can I come?" So I took her with me. I saw couple people up there still. Me and Monique went to a party. Elijah was there, he was watching me ALL night, every time someone came near me, he just stared at them, like a proper deadly stare. We got back to mine at 3.30am. Someone phoned when I got in, mom was cussin' asking how people can be calling the house phone those times of night. But by the time I went to answer it they'd put it down. I pressed 1471 but it said the number was withheld.

4th Jan 1998
Today we all cleaned the yard. I've ironed the uniforms, had a bath, and packed my school bag. So, everything's

sorted for school tomorrow. I wanted to oil my hair but there was no Blue Magic left and I hate using Dax, its green and thick; I aint putting that in my hair. Elijah came up (I was still in my nightie and my hair was a mess), I asked him if he would pick me up from school tomorrow, he said "do I look like a taxi?" Then he said "what time do you finish?" He knows! He dropped his phone in water so he said I should call one of his friends to get in touch with him.

I phoned Trayvon today, Lashelle and Nyah were there. What's Lashelle doing at Trayvon's? She's up to something I swear. I remember last year, around May, Lashelle kept asking for his number. Is she fukin him now? That gyal is sly you know. L'Neisha's in Jamaica, so now Trayvon's got them gyal up in his flat, what's that about?

5th Jan 1998

Today I picked up Chana from Sonia's. Chana was happy to see me, the little joker. As soon as I got back home we went food shopping, when I was there I saw Elijah, Shola, and the twin baby girls. No wonder he didn't pick me up from school. FUKIN HELL I DIDN'T REALISE SHE WAS THAT FAR GONE TO THE POINT THE TWINS WERE BORN. ELIJAH HAS JUST PLAYED THIS WHOLE THING DOWN. WE WALKED PAST EACH OTHER LIKE STRANGERS! Why didn't I call him out, why didn't I say something, why didn't I make Shola know he still calls me, and we still link? Oh yeah, if she finds out she'll kill herself and probably the babies too. I better not say anything.

Nothing else has really happened today. Elijah hasn't phoned me or been round. Times are too cold to go out, weathers freezing and gyal like me are just chillin'.

Kim phoned me today, I told her not to chat to me again. She's a rarse liar. She was crying and saying how she was sorry, but I can't be dealing with all the shit that comes with being her friend. She was trying to get me to lie to Kath 'bout that weed and money for her. No way, I didn't even know she was holding anything for him, so I aint getting involved. Me and her are done now, im not interested in anything she's got to say.

6th Jan 1998
Elijah hasn't phone me today and I haven't phoned him either. Jade came up here with her mom today, they've gotta move outta town. Her mom's ex has found out where she lives and apparently he used to beat them up. So now they're on the run. Some mad shit. I feel sorry for them, seems like they're always on the run from him. I wonder how he's found out where they live. Jades gonna have to move school and her mom might not be able to finish the next part of her nursing course at New Way Hospital. We might not see them for ages now, thank God.

I cleaned up for Gaynor today, she paid me £15. She was giving me joke telling me that when she was younger she lived on a council estate like me, I think she said it was called Park Hill. She said her family were one of the first families that had outdoor toilets and water, I didn't realise she was that old. She was telling me that she would go to bed scared most nights because there was loads of crime in that area of Yorkshire. MADNESS.

7th Jan 1998
School was ok today. Me, Lashelle, and Chana went to town. I saw couple of the Rising Star manz. They're jokers. I've told everyone it's my birthday soon. I'd really like

some trainers off my mom, and I'd like to spend the day with my dad doing something (not just shopping). A proper day out somewhere. Doubt that will happen though. Still aint seen Elijah, bastard. I saw his friend in town today, I said to him, if he sees Elijah tell him to phone me.

I was supposed to phone Louise back, but I forgot, she won't mind though 'cause she's probably with Scary-B teaching him a few more lessons!

I wanna go Shouters to celebrate my birthday.

8th Jan 1998
Today I went town after school. I saw couple people. Elijah phoned me, it's the first time we've spoken since I saw him and his little family out food shopping, I asked him what that was all about, he said she needed nappies. I said I weren't feeling his lies. We had one piece of argument, he asked me what my problem was and that I mustn't run up my mouth over foolishness. He eventually put the phone down on me. We spoke again later once he'd calmed down. I told him I'd meet him tomorrow.

11th Jan 1998
This is a summary of the whole weekend: Elijah slept here on Friday night. On Saturday morning his car wouldn't start, so he didn't leave here till 3pm. We had to push start the car, do I look like I know anything 'bout cars? I made him a chicken burger sandwich while he was here. He winked at me as if to say, 'thank you'.

Anyway, on Saturday, I didn't go anywhere at all. Couple people phoned me. Monique begged her mom to make her come in at 11:45pm, Marcia allowed it as well. Lucky bitch.

Today (Sunday) me, mom, Chana, and Janay all went to watch 'George in the Jungle' at the cinema and then we went to the Pizza Hut for dinner. It was nice that we all went out, wish we did it more often, but moms touring takes over. Anyway its 10:50pm, got school tomorrow.

12th Jan 1998

We met up with Elijah and his friends at Midpoint. I had a couple drinks, other than that the day was dry.

13th Jan 1998

Today at 7:30am I skived school and met Elijah. We went to his friends flat. We were up there for ages. He doesn't believe that I've only banged three people, including him. He was screwin' when I told him that Trayvon was one of them. He kept talking about Shola and the twins today, no disrespect but don't talk 'bout them when your around me.

I left the flat at 3pm and I hung around the depot until school was finished.

I phoned Monique; I've given her the lingwa. She couldn't believe that I went to meet Elijah at 7.30am and skived school.

14th Jan 1998

Them lot from school came round here to get my R.E book so they could catch up on some work. I called Monique; we were on the phone for ages. Good job its free. Cable to Cable!!
IMANI FOR ELIJAH
4-EVA

15th Jan 1998
Elijah phoned me today he's a joker. He asked if I was going to see him today. I said nah I was just staying in. He didn't say anything, normally he would cuss, must have been in one of his good moods! I've caught up with all my homework today too so that's good. I phoned Monique, she was telling me how her mom is going to be working away for a bit; she's campaigning for this thing called 'Take your daughter to work day', she wants it to be massive.

I've told bare people it's my birthday so I'm looking a good raise.

19th Jan 1998
My Birthdays been ok, I'm 15 today. JHEEZE. Everyone at school said happy birthday etc. I also got a card off the people in my class. Mom gave me £50, I bought some black stretch jeans, a blue cardigan, and a gold top. Money done. Nina and dad dropped off some money, they didn't even bother with a card. OH, and Uncle Vincent didn't get me a present (like he said he would). I remember at Xmas when he got Janay and Chana those gifts, he said I'd get something for my birthday, well I aint seen nothing. Didn't think I would anyway.

31st Jan 1998
Its 11pm. I haven't wrote in ages, so here goes...I've seen Elijah every day, every week etc. We always phone or see each other. He's picked me up from school a few times (that gave everyone at school something to talk about, including the teachers).

Elijah's always at my house, not that it bothers me. He's stayed here couple times on the weekend and I've stayed with him at his friends flat. For some reason Elijah thinks I've got nex' man, we've had some big arguments about it, but we've sorted it out now. He's taken my address book off me and said I had too much manz numbers. He really thinks I'm with someone else. All this is starting to pisssssssssss me off. He acts like he's innocent. He's the one with twin baby girls. But I still like him though.

Mom went to Belgium today, the group is doing well, and they might even be on MTVBase, not sure how long she's going for this time. Sometimes I wish she would tell us because then I could count the days down, but I think she likes to surprise us when she gets back.

I went for a job interview today as a telephonist (its fat money).

Our phone bill came the other day its £83.00. MAD business. SHIT. I've gotta come up with half of the money for dat.

Monique's had to take the morning after pill again. MADNESS

1st Feb 1998
Today I went for a trial run at work. It was tiring and a lot of people weren't interested, no-one wants windows, doors, and conservatories! This telesales ting is shit. I worked 10:30-3:15pm. I went back to Gaynor's nyamed some food and dropped Chana to Sonia's. I can't even bare to look Sonia the slag in the face. I phoned Elijah; he came up for a

bit. He went to McDonalds he bought me a cheeseburger, he kept saying I should order proper food, but I didn't wanna seem craven, so I said I'd have the cheeseburger! I'm back at Gaynor's chilling out.

I've been with Elijah for roughly 6 months, I aint doing too bad. He was saying how it's a privilege for me to be with him and how I'm lucky, I said do you regret getting with me, he said "I never said I regretted it." Like what the fuk does that really even mean. It wasn't the answer I was hoping for but it's the one I got. I do fancy him a lot, I don't think it's love though, I better not tell him that though. He asked me what makes me like him so much, I said I didn't even know. Imani are you stupid, why do I always say I don't know?

Monique thinks that she's pregnant. I've told her she needs to do a test asap.

2nd Feb 1998

Today's been one of those days, school was SHIT. I didn't get home from school till after 6pm, I stayed behind to talk to the Food Tech teacher about the recipe I'm gonna cook for tomorrow's lesson. She was telling me that I didn't have time to wash the chicken during the lesson and that even if I did she'd mark me down because washing chicken was unnecessary. Is she mad? She tried to say that washing chicken before cooking it increases the risk of food poisoning from bacteria. I had to tell her straight, round here we wash our meat and that I aint dissin' my culture for no GCSE. I can't even imagine what mom or dad would do if I told them I didn't wash my chicken, musi mad. I don't know anything different. We agreed that I can 'swill

139

it under the tap'! She thinks I'm just washing it under the tap, listen I'm bringing in my lemon and vinegar. I can't wait to see her face in the lesson, it's gonna be pure joke.

After school I went to Nyah's to look through some recipe books she said she had. Her aunt Nzinga was trying to tell me to cook some jollof rice. Yooooo does she want me to get dissed at school tomorrow, no way. Who's bussin African recipes, must be mad.

After Nyah's I went to work, I blagged my National Insurance number so hopefully my pay will be sorted out.

Monique phoned me today and told me that someone in her family had a dream about fish and that it means someone's pregnant. She's fully bummy now. Monique's told her man that she could be pregnant, and apparently he seemed all cool about it. She said he kept asking what *she* gonna' do, like she even knows at this point. She said that he hugged her and said that everything would be ok and there was no need for her to worry. If only Monique could start her period tomorrow or even Wednesday, she'd be safe.

3rd Feb 1998
Today was pressure, everyone has been asking me if I've heard that Monique's pregnant. How do they know? Who else has she told? My head's gonna explode, maybe I was being paranoid, but I swear everything about today felt like pregnancy or baby talk. It's starting to make me feel like it's *me* that's chatted her business, but I know it aint. Monique hasn't even done a test yet.

The Food Technology lesson was joke. I took out the lemon and the vinegar ready to wash the chicken and the teacher came round telling me she'll only allow me to swill it under the tap. I made out like I couldn't hear her; she was going mad saying she's gonna put me in detention. Detention for washing chicken, that will go down in history, these teachers are narsty. They haven't got a clue about our culture; when we went to Central station I wish that I'd suggested more black teachers coming in to teach the other teachers about our culture instead of making us feel like aliens 'cause we wash our fukin meat and use seasonings.

She gave me a D- for my chicken lasagne, saying it was over-seasoned and the chicken didn't need washing! But I know it tasted sweet, so I didn't business. I was selling it a dinnertime for £1 a slice, I made at least £12 today, a nice little raise.

Lashelle's trying to get things out of me about Monique, she can fuk off, prick. I told Monique, I had to. She's proper stressing. I asked her who else she'd told, but she said just me and him, well he must be chattin' her business 'cause it aint me. Elijah came to mine (6:30pm) he was here till 7:30pm, then he said he was going to 'lick a shot', not sure what that meant. He came back up at 8:30pm. He was telling me he wants a card and a diamond ring for valentines' day. Ha, I don't know where he thinks that moneys coming from. Dickhead. He said I better buy it, or else. Or else what?? Joker! He said he might buy me some chocolate. 'Might?' I know he aint buying me shit. Fukin chocolate, who the fuk wants chocolate. I told him I'm not buying any card, he asked why, I said because Shola might see. He said I could write it anonymously and he'll style it out like someone sent it to him through the post. What the fuk, like seriously is this what he really wants me to do? DICKHEAD.

4th Feb 1998

Time 11:05pm. Today a few of us went to Midpoint Youth Club. It was OK. After Midpoint I phoned Elijah, he told me to call him back in an hour, I never phoned back a rarse, couldn't be bothered. No doubt he's gonna go mad when I see him. Heard Ebony had a fight in town with some outta town gyal, apparently she bruked all three of them up. Three against one and she still fuked them all up.

5th Feb 1998

Elijah gave me a lift home from school today. He bought me a McDonalds; he's been really nice to me today.

Nina phoned me today asking if I was ok and beggin' me not to tell dad that she thinks he's had an affair with Sonia, I told her I weren't getting involved. She apologised for bringing me in to it, in true Nina style she said "Imani, I sincerely apologise for embroiling you with your fathers and I's marital concerns, this is not what you should be exposed to," she's a joker. To be honest I'd kinda forgot 'bout all that.

6th Feb 1998

Never went to school, I was in no mood. Elijah came round and we ordered dial-a-pizza. I wanted chicken, but he wanted ham, so we had to have ham. He always gets what he wants. Louise and Lashelle came round at dinner time. Guess what, I've been with Elijah all this time and didn't realise he sells cocaine. I heard him say the other day that he's going to 'lick a shot', I asked him what that meant, and he said, "babes you know I sell coke don't you?" ERRRRRRRR NO I DID NOT. I thought he was joking at first, like trying to wind me up, then I realised he was actually being serious. I thought it was a bit of weed if anything. I was like, what the fuk, he just started laughing. He was shocked that I didn't know. This just gets better, fukin coke you know. I said maybe we should finish 'cause it aint about being with a drug dealer, he was like, babes stop being stupid. So, I guess we aint done then. He was telling me that Shola is fired, and I'm hired. He's a joker. He said he just wants to be there for his daughters and that he aint with her. Not sure I believe him. He tells too many lies. He said they've finished for good this time.

7th Feb 1998

I worked 10-2pm today. Then I came home. Elijah came up after I finished work, he's really been pissin' me off today to be honest. He's been dragging me by my hair and all sorts (Bastard) he makes out like it's a joke and just fun. NOTHINGS FUNNY ABOUT IT. Why does he pretend it's a game? He said it's his way of showing me he loves me, that sounds like a load of crap to me. Afterwards we went bowling, he bought me some snacks. He kept putting his arm round me and telling me I was his girl, it felt nice. He was telling me that for Valentine's Day he might buy me a watch and some earrings, I'll believe that when I see it. He aint buying me shit. Loves talking 'bout might this and might that'. How 'bout you 'do' something, all chat and no rarse action.

8th Feb 1998

Went to work, was meant to meet Elijah afterwards in the bus station but he didn't turn up. If this was the other way round, I'd never hear the end of it, but its ok for him to do it to me though. GRRR. When I was in the bus station I saw Queen Cartel Squad arguing with some girls from outta town, it looked like they were gonna start a fight. They were outing their cigarettes on the girls arms, that must have hurt badly man. They're horrible. Elijah phoned me when I got in around 4pm asking if I want to meet up with him. I said no, I asked him why he didn't meet me earlier, he said he forgot, and I must stop watching his every move like a hawk. He called me back at 7pm to see if I had changed my mind. I said no, he said I was an ignorant bitch and that out of all the girls he could call, I should be grateful it was me. Ohhh pleaseee, FUK OFF and call them then. Aint in the mood to see him, he's annoying me at the moment.

9th Feb 1998

After school I went to work to pick up my wage packet. Then I went to the family planning clinic with Monique. She finally had a pregnancy test, it was positive. When the woman told her the results she just burst into tears man. I didn't even know what to say to her. We walked back to the bus station in silence.

Elijah came here at 9pm and left at 11:45pm. I asked if he was gonna apologise for being so wrenk yesterday, he started laughing and said I was too sensitive and that he was only joking. I told him that Monique was pregnant (everyone else knows 'bout it so I didn't think it was that bad to tell him) he didn't say much except, 'what she gonna do? I told him she wasn't sure.

I'm applying for a job at Cold Press Windows, it pays more than where I am now, so fingers crossed I get that one. From this day forward gyals like me are going on the pill, I can't be taking them hot moves like Monique anymore. I can't believe my best friends pregnant, like shit man.

The Puff Daddy concert is definitely cancelled, it isn't going to be on the 14th Feb.

1st March 1998

Aint wrote in here for ages, loads been going on lately.
We went Woodberry, when we were there we saw someone that looked like Winston, Chana's dad. From the back it looked like him anyway, quite tall with broad shoulders. I thought it can't be him anyway 'cause he works away in the Army, what would he be doing in Woodberry? Two twos, the person turned around and I could tell it was him, he had a baby on his chest in one of those baby carrier/slings. This could never be his pikni. I said "Janay, isn't that Winston." Janay walked straight over and said, "is this what you do when you tell Chana you're busy working away in the Army, gallivant up and down shopping with your new yeute?" He couldn't say one word, Janay made him look like a fool, then this woman came walking out the shop asking Janay to calm down because she's gonna wake up her baby. Janay said, "do you know he's got a 10-year- old kid, our sister who he does not see?" The woman was like WHAT. She never knew anything about Chana. Winston was stood there like some dyam arse. Me and Janay just walked off, we were deciding whether to tell mom or Chana or both. We decided to loawe it, Winston aint in Chana's life enough for it to make any

difference, he's wukless either way. We told him not to come back to the house EVER again either. He better not. DICKHEAD.

2nd April 1998
Dad's Birthday
Schools been so intense lately, bare coursework and stuff, I've not even had chance to write in my diary. Dads birthday today and after last year when I made him the handmade card I decided I wasn't getting him fuk all this year. No time for ungrateful people, dad or not. I can't be arsed. Nina called at 7pm, I couldn't be arsed to talk to her, so I made out like I had to go and clean up. I wonder if she was gonna ask me what I'd got dad for his birthday or something.

21st April 1998
Aint wrote in here for ages, just been feeling low lately. I can't really explain it but just a weird feeling. Everything seems to piss me off, and I can't really explain why. I feel like my heads gonna explode most of the time, I aint got anyone to really talk to. I can talk to Gaynor, she's cool, but she's not exactly my age. I don't feel like I've really got anyone to talk to about how I'm feeling. I don't even know what it is I'd say anyway, everything feels like it's getting on top of me, school, Elijah, dad, Nina, Monique's problems, plus all the other shit going on in my head.

23rd April 1998
Today I went to work. I came back home and was just chillin' then my DAD comes MARCHING round. Some chatty mout' persons told him 'bout me and Elijah. He was going mad. I can't be bothered to explain all the details. He

146

told me to finish with Elijah and that I shouldn't be having any man. After he left, Elijah phoned me, I told him that we need to dun, he asked why. I just said I couldn't be bothered to explain. I can't believe me and him are actually finished. When dad came down, Nina the bitch was with him. That made things even worse. She was standing there like a smug twat. Her hair scraped in her dumb ponytail; I should have yanked it round my wrist. BITCH. She didn't show any emotion, probably scared that she might ruin her make up. She didn't even tell my dad to calm down or anything.

24th April 1998

Today I went to work, you never guess who I saw in reception waiting for an interview, Ebony. I couldn't believe it!! It's about time she looked for work, she can't be trying to tax people all her life. I wonder if she'll get the job. Chana slept at Sonia's tonight. It still grieves me to think that she's seeing my dad and fren's
us all up like I don't fukin know, the tramp.

25th April 1998

Today I went to work, I only picked up
£37. Afterwards I went into town.
Monique didn't come, she said
she was feeling sick. Dad said
how we (me, Chana, and Janay)
have to go round Sonia's as
from tomorrow because Gaynor
aint looking after us properly.
He said she's too old to be watching and keeping an eye on us and how we're all just taking the piss.

26th April 1998

Today I bought most of my stuff to Sonia's. I've been round here since 4pm. Today's been dry as fuk. This may seem silly, but I never thought I'd see the day when I say, "I MISS ELIJAH."

Sitting in the same room as sly Sonia makes me sick. She acts all nice like she's just helping mom out by looking after us, how would mom feel if she knew her best friend was sleeping with her ex. I know mom and dad aint together; but come on man, Sonia aint got any morals, the slag.

27th April 1998

Today I went to school. Nothing exciting happened. I went to work. Ebony started today; she was sitting a few rows in front of me getting trained by this mixed race girl. I've never seen Ebony so quiet. I never got the job at Cold Press Windows, so I'm staying at this place for now. I work every day 4pm-8:30pm and on a Saturday 10-2pm. I don't work on Sundays. This is my sixth week. Hopefully, I should be getting £97 on Saturday. My bank account is going to be fat. I'm going to try and save at least £350 this year MAX. I'll spend the rest on shoes and shit. I phoned the bank and I've arranged for them to send me a monthly statement, the 1st of every month. Today has been pissin' down with rain. Nothing else has happened.

Tuesday 28th April 1998

I can't believe its Tuesday; it feels like a Thursday. Anyway, today has been ok. I went school but left at dinnertime, couldn't be bothered to do the whole day.

I went to work, and I got two leads. One blew out in fact they both did. I don't know why people say they'll have a free window quotation when we call, but then when it goes to second stage, they change their minds, I'm on commission, these people need to stop cancelling. GRRRRRRRRR.

I think it's time I wrote about Monique being pregnant. Well, she had sex with her man (obviously) and the condom split. I went family planning with her for the morning after pill. After a while she said she knew she was pregnant, she said she could just feel it somehow. After about six weeks we went back. She did a pregnancy test; it came up positive. She couldn't believe it, nor could I. After that I had to keep skiving school to go to the doctors with her. I wasn't going to make her go through all that on her own, you mad. Monique wanted an abortion so they gave her an appointment.

It was at The Williamson Clinic. She had to ask her older cousin Leanne to go with her, they wouldn't do it unless someone over the age of 18 gave consent. There's no way she could tell her mom; Marcia campaigns for women's rights and is pro-life. She would never have made Monique have that abortion. We skived school and I met Monique at 9am in the bus station. From there we caught the train; me, her and Leanne all went together. We got there about 12pm. We were waiting around for ages. Then they called her upstairs to theatre, me and her cousin had to wait in the waiting room.

At about 4:15pm we were allowed to go in to see her, she was in a room, it looked like a normal bedroom. We were worried for her; we weren't sure what we should say when we saw her. When we went into her room, she was sitting up, which surprised me. I thought she'd be lying down but she looked fine. I asked how she was, and she said she felt ok. She was telling us that she just remembers having an injection in the back of her hand and being told to count to 10, then waking up like nothing had happened. She said that she was hungry because she hadn't been allowed to eat anything since midnight the day before, except water. I remember when I went with her to the doctors and he was saying that if she ate anything on the day of the appointment then they wouldn't be able to carry out the abortion. Just as she was saying that this lady -probably a nurse came round and asked her if she wanted some toast. Monique said yes. When the Nurse left, she was giving us some joke, she was saying she was looking some chicken and rice 'bout they're trying to give her toast!! We were all laughing, but then this other woman came in and asked us to keep the noise down because other 'ladies' were trying to rest. There weren't any other 'ladies', everyone else on the ward looked the same age as us, or a bit older. Just seeing the way the nurses were working and how they were really trying to help Monique makes me know that I'd love to do that for a job, fuk what Jade and Kim's mom think, I'm gonna be a Nurse.

Me and her cousin left at 5pm. The next morning, we did the same long ass train journey to go and get her. Monique was saying that once we left her, she spent the rest of the evening eating chicken and chips, watching Ricky Lake and talking to this other girl that was in the bed opposite hers. I'm glad they gave her something proper to eat.

Anyway, my hands hurting me. More details tomorrow.

29th April 1998

Same old routine, school, and work. Nothing exciting has happened today. I got a bonus of £10 for two immediate leads at work today. Ebony asked if I could share my bonus with her, is she mad?? Does she know how many phone calls it took to get that lead. So now she's stopped taxing and has started to ask to 'share'!! She's slowly learning isn't she!! Wonder how long it'll take for her to just STOP begging altogether.

I phoned Monique to see how she was, she seemed fine. She was telling me that the abortion she had is known as a suction or vacuum abortion. Basically, she said, they suck the baby out of the womb. I didn't even know there was more than one type of abortion. I can't believe how casual she was talking about it, maybe I thought she would be more emotional, quiet, or upset, but she seemed like her normal self.

30th April 1998

Today I've been feeling in a pissed off mood. At school tipex spilled in my bag and on my uniform. Then I thought I lost my folder with my Science coursework, but then I remembered where it was. I got a lead at work today, so I suppose that was good. When I got home from school I needed to bake some biscuits for tomorrows Food Tech lesson. The first batch I cooked were messed up, so it's taken all evening. I never phoned Monique today. I hope she doesn't think I don't care about her, she seemed fine yesterday when I spoke to her so hopefully she'll be ok.

Elijah phoned stressing my head, saying he misses me, and we should carry on seeing each other. He said no-one needs to know, why does he never take no for an answer. He said that I should do what I want and that I shouldn't let people dictate my life, the irony.

Today has been a stressed-out day.
I'm tired.

1st May 1998

Today was OK, school and work were good. I got about 3 leads so I should get some decent bonuses. The minimum I should pick up next week should be £65.

Anyway, I phoned Elijah today, he couldn't stay on the phone long he had to 'lick a shot'. I hate when he uses that phrase, especially now that I know exactly what it means. When he phoned me back later I asked him why he couldn't just get a normal job and why he was selling drugs. He said that his mom's only a dinner lady and that money was tight. He said that his dad left his mom when he was a yeute, so he had to be the man of the house now and that there was no way he was gonna make his mom struggle. I hear that still.

2nd May 1998

Today I went to work. I got paid £94. I was gonna sneak and meet Elijah at 5pm (but I couldn't be arsed and if I got caught by anyone it would just be headache.) He called me but I never answered the phone because he would've got mad that I didn't go and see him. Me and Chana went out, everyone loves when I bring her with me she's such a little character, she makes everyone laugh with her dancing and singing. I got back to Sonia's at 10pm. That's it really, oh I went to town and I saw the Queen Cartel Squad bullying some girls that had come down from outta town, they're fukry man. If anyone comes to the area that aint from round here they wanna beat them up or tax them.

3rd May 1998

I stayed in until 4:30pm. All this shit is messed up with Elijah, so I decided to phone Trayvon; he said L'Neisha was on her way up but that she was leaving at 11pm. I didn't even know she was back in the country, last I heard she was still in Jamaica visiting family. He asked me what time I had to be in, in other words, he wanted me to come up after she had left. KISS MY TEETH.

Anyway, I looked good yesterday with my Reebok classics Jheeze

4th May 1998

Monique's Birthday.
Today I went to work 11-3 pm. I didn't get any leads. Afterwards I went to Trayvon's, even though we don't link anymore we're still close. As I was leaving, L'Neisha came up. She didn't say anything to me though. Some hot moves. I passed by Monique's house for a bit too, we didn't do much, we just chilled at hers and drank some Alize and a couple Bacardi Breezers.

5th May 1998

School was alright. I was telling Nyah about me going Trayvon's yesterday. Nyah said that Lashelle was begging to know what we were on a bout. Lashell's too in my business.

7th May 1998

Today I never went school, it was elections. Work was so shit today, no leads man.

After work I phoned Trayvon, he said L'Neisha was trying to say he'd done a ting with me when she saw me going to his flat the other day. My gyals paranoid'. Why didn't she say something when she saw me then? I never touched him, well not that day anyway!! He was telling me that he might go to Jamaica with L'Neisha in the school holidays, it's like that then yeah. Okayyyyyyyyy.

I heard Caleb is out of the penn. Can't believe he's been in there since August 97, mad how the times flown by. I wonder if he'll settle his skin now and not get into trouble with the feds. Trayvon will be buzzin' to have his right hand man back on the road.

8th May 1998

I got up at 11am, got dressed and cleaned up. I went to my own house at 12:30pm. I met Lashelle at 2pm. I hate staying at Sonia's, I can't stand sly people.

I never phoned Monique today. I'll sneak a call to her from work tomorrow.

Saw Caleb A.K.A Devious, he's fresh out the penn. He's gone massive, he was saying that prison was mad and that he just used to pump weights all day. He was telling us how the routine in there was annoying. He said nuff man he knows are inside, so it wasn't that bad, everyone looked out for each other. Sounds like Midpoint to be fair, youth club for criminals! He was telling us that he doesn't wanna go back in, so he's gonna try get on a college course and keep out of trouble.

9th May 1998
GAYNORS BIRTHDAY

It's exactly a year since I got Gaynor that book about forgiveness, I didn't know what to get her this year, so I went round and asked what she wanted. The cancers come back, she was saying how she just wants to live. She was telling me that I should live my life the way that I want to and to do what I can while I can because we only live once. I swear I've heard that before from someone else, can't think who.

I asked Gaynor if she ever sent off the letter that she started to write to her daughter Eileen, she said it was still upstairs on her bedside cabinet.
A whole year later.

I've got a plan.

Today work was shit, we got <u>no</u> leads. I picked up £67. I put £40 in the bank. Elijah phoned me; he wants me to go to his house tomorrow. WORD. We aint even meant to be chattin', let alone meeting each other. I said no, and he said that I need to stand up for myself and stop making other people tell me how to live my life. How weird coming from him!!

10th May 1998

Today I've been at my own house most of the day. The time's 22:59. I'm listening to Destiny's Child 'No, no, no', the tune is dark. Monique came up to mine today. We were runnin' pure joke. Elijah phoned me at 5pm, he asked me to come to his, so to shut him up I said I would. At 8:30pm he phoned and asked where I was! At first he was going mad, telling me I better get in a taxi and get to his house, I was a bit scared. Then he calmed down, me and him were on the phone for ages. We were talking about the old times, then as usual I said something that he didn't agree on and we started arguing. I just put the phone down. He phoned back at 10pm (man was still begging me to go and meet him). I miss him, but I don't want no shit in my ears from my dad. Mom phoned me today, she told me to try do work experience in the Civic Centre if I can. Civic Centre- office work. Nahh, I wanna be a Nurse or a Chef, not sit in some dry ass office all day. Next time mom calls I'll see what she thinks about me being a Nurse.

11th May 1998

Today I went to school and work. Everyone was saying that Ebony was gonna get sacked when she came in today. The Manager has had bare complaints about her. Apparently when she's been calling people asking if they want windows and doors, she's been saying 'my manager will call you back to confirm so you better not change your mind!' How she gonna be threatening people on the phone, I swear she's too much. If she gets sacked, she'll probably go back to taxing everyone in the depot like she used to do.

I never phoned Monique either, couldn't be arsed to chat to anyone today, got my own shit to sort. My life's a mess and I aint in the mood to be calling anyone right now. Came home and washed my hair. It looks kriss, some proper sheen business.

Louise told me how Parminder (one Indian gyal from school who thinks that she's hot) lost her virginity to Sunil. Jokers. Make their parents hear, they'll be sent on the first plane outta here, ha, ha.

Anyway, Lata on.

12th May 1998
Went work. Elijah's been on my case 'bout meeting up so I went and met him. I got back to Sonia's at 1am. Sonia was going mad saying how she's told my dad that I'm lazy and how I don't do anything in the house. Errrrrr well that's a blatant lie, I do stuff in the house. Dad phoned when I got in, he said he's going to buss my arse tomorrow. Shall I run away tonight and leave a note? I should tell them that I know what they've both been up to behind Nina's back, let's see who they wanna shout at then. I'll fuk up everyone's world.

13th May 1998
Dad came round here at 6am. I know he's an early bird but even 6am is early, I wonder if he slyly stayed here during the night?

He said I aint got no shame. Then he said how I don't do anything for Chana. Is he mad? I do pure stuff for Chana. It's not his business anyway, Chana aint even his kid, so why's he so concerned. How's Sonia the slag sitting on the top of the stairs in her dumb fukin red satin pyjamas and making him cuss me, I can't believe it. I know they're definitely fukin each other. Tramps. I should have told them I know their narsty little secret and mashed up everything.

When's mom coming back. She's been on tour since the end of January. Fuk me, I might run away you know, give them something to fukin worry 'bout then. Coming in at 1am is nothing compared to what I can do. The way I feel half the time they're lucky I aint done it already. What if I kill myself, huh? What then. Dickheads. He said in my school holidays I have to go and stay with him and Jehovah witness juice drinking Nina. I aint gonna go if I can help it.

14th May 1998

Today I went to work. At 6:30pm, one of my managers closed the office. He came in and said the business wasn't doing very well and that today was our last day. We all left. I couldn't believe it. Me and Lashelle went to Midpoint. All dem manz were down there. I banged Elijah at his house, no-one was in. That'll teach my dad for thinking he can fukin tell me what to do, we didn't use anything you know either, fuk it I don't care.

I aint telling anyone that the Manager closed the tele-sales office.

15th May 1998

Janay is so nosey. At school Lashelle told me how she overheard Alisha and Janay talking. Janay was saying how she was looking for some socks in my drawer, then she saw a book and it had about Monique being pregnant, so she read it.

A BOOK??
NO IT WASN'T A RANDOM BOOK, ITS THIS DIARY, BOUT A BOOK.

Anyway, after school, me and Lashelle went to Elijah's. We left around 8:30pm, we were there from 5:30pm. I got in at 9:15pm. Nuen did gwarn, I was on my reds. I'm starting to take the pill again. Elijah wants me to meet him at 2pm outside McDonalds (that's a hot move) we'll see tomorrow.

16th May 1998

Today I went to get my final cheque from work. I heard that Ebony's wages have been docked 'cause of all the complaints that were made about her from the customers. The managers have said if she wants to get her cheque she has to write a letter of apology to ALL the customers she had up. Serves her right, it's about time she was made to apologise, especially with the amount of people that's she's taxed and bullied over the years. Hopefully, she'll realise that what goes around comes around. BRUTE.

17th May 1998

I went to Imogen's, she's back from Greece. I can't believe it's been 9 months already since they went. She was telling me all about Greece and how she was staying in this place called Santorini if that's how you even spell it. She said the weather was proper hot every day and she lived right by the beach. She said the family that her mom was looking after were proper rich and they gave Imogen anything she wanted. She said the food out there is nice as well. Imogen was saying that her mom is thinking of living out there. It's got more opportunities for her and Imogen. So, it looks like they might be moving to Greece. I told her she could be my pen pal!! I sometimes want to ask her 'bout lipsing Dejuan, but I just think nah, forget it. That was in the past.

I need a job real quick, I haven't told anyone about the office closing, so they still think that I go to work every day, ha, ha, don't watch me!!!
Anyway, Lata on.

18th May 1998
After school me and Louise went to town, she saw Scary-B he gave her £20. BLOODCLART. Those lessons she's been giving him really been paying off!!

Parents evening was the same, bare good reports. Sonia wanted to come with me true moms still not back, but I asked Gaynor instead. She looked really tired today, but she still said she'd come with me. I aint trying to walk up and down smiling with Sonia and she's up to her fukry, no way. When I was at Gaynor's she kept going to the toilet, frig knows what she doing in there so often. One of the times when she went into the bathroom, I sneaked into her room and found the letter that she had started to write to Eileen. I pushed it in my bra, I'm gonna add some more stuff to it and post it.

Oh, Nyah's going to America or Africa (ha) in the six weeks holiday with her Aunt Nzinga, they can eat as much jollof rice as they want to there. Ha, ha.

Oh, yesterday when I was at Imogen's she was telling me that her and her mom are going back to Greece to start looking at houses and that they were going in the six weeks holiday.

19th May 1998

Saw Elijah he was being alright. We've kinda sorted things out. We were having a good conversation, about 'us'. I lipsed him couple times. He was being nice to me. He said he liked me a lot. He told me he's banged Natalie. Dwayne was right wasn't he? I remember last year summer him telling me that he thought she had fuked out on him, no way. Wow. I wonder why Elijah thinks he can casually tell me 'bout linkin' nex gyal and that I'm meant to be just ok with it. Madness. Despite his bullshit, I've told him I'll tell everyone else we're finished but that I'd still link him. He said he'd get rid of all his other girls and that I'd made it to number one. Got in at 11pm, pure cuss from my dad (again), he was already at Sonia's when I got there. Either she called him and told him I hadn't got back yet, or he was there anyway. Sly bastards.

Fukin vicious cycle, you cuss me, I get mad; I do what I want, you cuss me more. DON'T THESE ADULTS GET IT??? He said I have to go and stay with him and Nina on Sunday for my half term holiday. FUKIN HELL. That's not the flex, third time this month he's had to speak to me.

Get me outta this house...

20th May 1998

I tried to phone Monique, but she wasn't back from school. Mom phoned today, she seems like she's having a good time, lucky for some. Can't wait for her to come back. Aint seen her since January, this is mad. Went Midpoint Youth Club, the usual people were there, we were ketchin some joke. I'm confused at the moment. Everyone seems to be telling me to loawe it with Elijah, but it aint that straight forward and no-one seems to get it. You can't just finish with him like that.

I finished the letter that Gaynor had started writing to Eileen and I posted it today, I'm begging that she writes back.

21st May 1998
I phoned Elijah after school (7pm) he was giving me joke. We were talking about the party that's coming up at Club Peach. Hopefully, I can go. Elijah said he'd pay me in if I go!! (we'll see). Oh, he was saying he might have to go to court soon; the other day he got arrested again (what's new). I don't want him to go to tha penn.

22nd May 1998
I stayed over at Louise's house (Sonia thought I was sleeping at my cousins) at about 12:30am we went to Rising Star Blues. I stayed out with Elijah till 6:30am.

23rd May 1998
I haven't slept properly. I went to sleep from 2:30pm until 7:30pm. Dad's back on my case. I swear he's meant to be doing property, go and check on your yards and leave me alone. Don't fukin come down when shit hits the fan. Where are you normally? Listen, no one get me mad. I'm going to my bed. Oh yeahh, Sonia's took my house keys off me. They know I didn't sleep at my cousins the other day (thanks to Janay and her big mouth). I'm not going to talk to Janay for a couple of weeks. Does she get a buzz out of being an informer, just 'cause her life's dry, she wants to mash up mine. No excitement's going on for her, so she wants to ruin my fun. True she doesn't know I saw those tablets in her drawer, I reckon there ecstasy tablets, unlike her I WONT be informing.

24th May 1998

Elijah's gonna kill me. He told me to call him as soon as I reached my dad's. Got here about 3:15pm. Its 10:15pm and I'm in bed. BORED. I hope he don't go mad that I aint called him. Nina was saying *"boys don't appreciate girls and that I should save myself for marriage and that the body is a wholly temple."* She was even saying that *"sex is a matrimony and the highest connection you can have with another being."* I'd switched off, all that posh talk doesn't work with me. Temple (isn't that where Hindus and Sikhs go?)

They're trying to force me to live up here after I leave school, but dat nah guh work. Dad gave me twenty quid; maybe he feels guilty and thinks money will make all the other shit disappear, I'll take your money but I aint forgot shit. Nina was saying how *"where you reside now Imani isn't a great environment'* and *'your environment is one of the greatest impacts on who you become."* FUK OFF NINA, just because you come from Cambridge you think you can diss my ends?? Then she was telling me that getting her PhD in Finance from Cambridge University was the best thing she ever done. CLAP. Stop trying to big up yourself, you've got a PhD in finance but you aint got any rarse sense. I'm here making you spend your money bitch!!! Then she was saying she wanted to raise me from a long time ago etc. Bitch you can't even raise your own son. My mom don't really have any dealings with Nina. I'm not sure if she likes her or not, but if I tell my mom that Nina wanted me to live with her, my mom will kick Nina down...all the way back to Cambridge where she came from. They're making out that I'm lonely and that's why I'm 'misbehaving' (according to them). I'm BEGGIN GOD NOT 2 MAKE ME LIVE UP HERE WITH THESE FUKERS.

I should be going shopping tomorrow, I'm gonna make Nina spend all her money, the dyam arse. Like how she feels sorry for me, I'll milk this shit.

25th May 1998
The times 21:32pm and I'm lying in bed. Today I was up from 9am. Nina came in the room asking if I want carrot or beetroot juice for breakfast. What kinda options are they. Yo, I just wanna egg sandwich and a hot chocolate. Carrot juice? She said that bread isn't good for me and how hot chocolate was filled with 'refined sugar'. I said I wasn't hungry in the end; 'cause I don't know WHO she's offering juice to for breakfast. At 2:30pm we went shopping, Nina spent about £500 on me, yeah man, that's right you spend your money, ha. I got pure stuff from Morgan, I got some shoes from Ravel (if you know then you know) and I got some stuff from Jane Norman too.

I phoned Elijah. He seemed happy to hear from me. He never got mad about me not calling sooner which was a relief. Today has been ok I suppose. I've seen some tick manz up here. Nina's been giving me another lecture about man, she knows I'm still linkin' Elijah, but she's not directly saying it. She said *"boys are only after spontaneous sex and that adolescent boys should be concentrating on schoolwork and their exams"* she said, *"adolescent boys lack grounding and morals because their fathers are absent and now they're seeking love from young girls."* Wooooooooooooo Nina, it's not that deep. Chill. We're teenagers having fun.

26th May 1998
We went shopping again, Nina bought me pure garms, some knee-high boots from Dolcis, White Musk perfume from The Body Shop, she even bought me a perfume, and

loads of CDs. This woman's got money. Is all this spending on me and bribery Godly? Monique phoned me at 9pm, we were on the phone for an hour, we were ketchin joke. She was telling me that she's heard Elijah's been arrested again, what's wrong with him?

I've watched Home and Away, The Bill, Ricky Lake and Emmerdale... boredom! I hate TV, but there's fuk all else to do down here, and at least Nina doesn't distract me when she thinks I'm watching TV.

27ᵗʰ May 1998

Nina has been pissin' me off today. She needs to piss off and go and read one of her Woman's Weekly magazines. Why isn't dad doing any of these 'silly little talks,' yo don't send Nina the beetroot drinking tramp to chat to me, I aint got nuen to say to her. Nina and dad must think having me here is gonna stop me living my life. This is what teenagers do, we have fun, we link man, we chat on the phone all day, we party. Didn't they do any of this as kids, come in like they're jealous or something, ha!

28ᵗʰ May 1998

Today Nina got me up at 7:30am, offering me ginger and lime water! I knew she was up early. I could hear the yoga music she plays blasting from the living room. I was screwing. She was telling me how ginger and lime is good for you and it flushes out toxins. No one cares, my woman aint right I swear. Just make me a hot chocolate and get out the room is all I was thinking. We went shopping again today. Nina's rinsing loads of money on me, yo my CD collection is looking heavy. She's bought me bare garms, can't wait to buss these when I get back home. I saw quite a few nice manz still. She bought me a personal stereo too.

30th May 1998

Today I've reached back home. Nina and dad drove me halfway then I jumped on the train the last part of the journey, they had business meetings so they couldn't drop me all the way home. I'm glad anyway, the thought of sitting in the car with both of them for hours on end would not be tha lique. Nina was going on about a new car she wanted and that her colleague has the V6 version, but she wants the V9, this woman is so follow-fashion it's a shame.

Dad said, "*yuh even know de difference between de two cars dem?*" Nina said, "I know ones newer and that's all that counts." What a fool. I just put in my headphones, what you know 'bout blanking a bitch. At the train station, say about ten minutes before my train came, while dad went to the toilet Nina was telling me how she had read my diary. She was barling. **I DIDN'T GIVE A FUK ABOUT HER CRYING.** She was saying that I'm in a domestic violence relationship with Elijah and that she's gonna get me some help. Is she mad? Domestic violence...nah let's not exaggerate the ting Nina. She was saying that the play fighting and stuff wasn't normal and that we should press charges. Is this woman out of her mind?? This is not a police ting. We don't call the feds for play fighting. Idiot. I begged her not to tell Dad. I told her it wasn't domestic violence. I'm not a battered housewife. She said "Imani, *it is Domestic violence, Elijah tries to gain power and control over you.*" I don't know why she's trying to call a few little scuffles domestic violence.

I hope she doesn't tell dad what she's read. **WHY THE FUK DO PEOPLE THINK ITS OK TO READ MY FUKIN DIARY THEN QUESTION ME ON MY FUKIN**

BUSINESS AND MY FEELINGS. IT'S MY PRIVATE FUKIN THOUGHTS-HOW DARE THEY. YOU WANNA READ MY BUSINESS THEN ASK ME ABOUT IT-GET THE FUK OUTTA HERE. I SHOULD HAVE SAID IT WAS ALL A LIE AND I WAS TESTING THEM TO SEE IF THEY WOULD READ IT. THAT WOULD HAVE BEEN FUNNY. THESE PEOPLE GOT NO FUKIN RESPECT FOR ME. AND THEY WONDER WHY I DON'T GIVE A FUK ABOUT THEM. LOVE TO INVADE AND VIOLATE MY SPACE. I knew that Nina was a bitch. What kinda Jehovah Witness is she? I swear it must say something in the bible about being nosey and invading peoples rarse space. She probably aint got to that part yet, tru she's just a recent convert. TWAT.

I need a little time to think things over.

On the train back, I sat and thought about what Nina was saying about it being domestic violence, I mean it's a bit far-fetched. That's when those women get battered in their houses and can't speak up for themselves; me and Elijah aint in anything like that. But it has got me thinking, is this how those domestic violence things start out? Should I talk to Gaynor, she'll know if its domestic violence or not. But true Gaynor's getting sicker I tend not to talk about my stuff anymore, I try and uplift her spirits and stuff. Don't want her worrying about me. You know something nah, Nina is just overreacting. Glad I won't be seeing them for a while.

31st May 1998

Went Riverside fair. 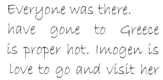 Everyone was there. Imogen and her mom have gone to Greece today, I bet over there is proper hot. Imogen is sooo lucky man. I'd love to go and visit her in Greece one day. I need to make sure I get her address so I can write to her.

1st June 1998.

Today's been a long ting. Everyone asks so many questions, Elijah this, Elijah that.

HE'S BEEN LOCK UP SINCE MAY, SO WHATS WITH ALL THE QUESTIONS
Life! Aint worth it.

2nd June 1998

Went to school at breaktime about 11:15am. Came home from school slept from 5pm-6:45pm then again from 8-11pm. Really feel low, stressed, violated, humiliated, worried, anxious. I can't believe Nina's read everything in here, is there any point in me carrying on this diary when everyone reads it anyway?

3rd June 1998

Went Midpoint, nuff people kept saying how my figure was tha lique etc. I'm sick of hearing it now, it used to make me feel sweet, now I can't be arsed.

10th June 1998

Saw couple of Trayvon's friends in town, they were telling me that Trayvon and L'Neisha are goin to Jamaica in a few weeks, she wants to introduce him to the rest of her family. Don't know what they're telling me for. Me and Trayvon aint been in anything for months. Good luck to both of them.

11th June 1998
Saw the Queen Cartel Squad in town, what do they favour. I'm gonna start calling them the banana crew, dem gyal need to invest in Colgate real quick or give up the fags' man, their teeth are YELLOW.

13th June 1998
Moms back today, yayyyyyyyyy. Me and Louise went to Midpoint; we were there from about 4pm till about 9pm. When I got back mom was getting ready to go to her friend's party, so I didn't really get to see her properly. At 10pm I went with Louise back to hers to get her stuff because she was gonna stay at mine. Didn't get back to mine till about 11:45pm.

14th June 1998
House phone is back on incoming calls, madness.

16th June 1998
Sports Day. What knob of a teacher decided that any gyal would wanna do sports day? Who the fuk decided to put this on the curriculum, no-one gives a fuk?

After Sports Day, Brianna was telling me how Lashelle was saying she doesn't know how I'm gonna ketch man in 'those shorts,' first of all there's no man to even ketch at school and secondly, I've never been in short of man looking at me so she needn't worry about my P.E shorts. DICKHEAD.

17th June 1998
Louise wasn't at school today which made dealing with Lashelles bullshit even harder. She was probably with Scary-B somewhere KISS MY TEETH.

20th June 1998
Saturday: Went to mom's friend's wedding.
Sunday: woke up at 6:30pm, seriously was knackered, the wedding mashed me up. I lipsed one boy at the wedding, don't even know his name. FUK ME. I had too many Bacardi Breezers. I think I had about 9 of them!
Popped in on Gaynor today, she's getting a bit weaker now and I can tell this cancer is trying to take over her body, she's lost bare weight.

22nd June 1998
School was shit. Yesterday was Nina's birthday I didn't call her or dad. Fuk them.

23rd June 1998
I went to school in the afternoon, it was shit. I'm glad I didn't do the full day. Louise was telling he how when she was lipsing Scary-B the other day, she was wanking him and spunk came off in her hand, I bet he felt shame! They never had any tissue, so she had to wipe it on her top!!

After school I popped in on Gaynor, she's getting worse; her skin is looking paler each time I see her. I go and see her quite often, but I don't always write about it in here. It makes me sad, and I start to feel the tears roll down my face, even now I can feel my eyes welling up. Eileen hasn't wrote back either so either she didn't get the letter or she's as stubborn as her mom, there's nothing else I can do.

170

24th June 1998
School finished at 1pm, I came home sorted out my homework and then went out.

25th June 1998
Stayed in till about 6pm, then went Louise's, we were drinking till about 1am. Can't even remember what else happened today.

26th June 1998
Got up at 3:30pm, that Vodka must have licked me yesterday. Mom's performing tonight, so she's out. I'm home, chillin, I wish I could see her perform. I'm gonna ask her if she can sing me one of her songs so I can hear what she sounds like. Would you believe I've never heard her sing, not properly anyway? I normally just hear her when she's practising her warmups, never like an actual song.

27th June 1998
I slept at Louise's tonight. Me, her, and Scary-B went cinema. It was ok. After the cinema, we went back to hers. I felt like a spare wheel. I should've just gone home.

28th June 1998
Got home about 6pm from Louise's. I chilled in. I heard that some of the Queen Cartel Squad have been caught bullying girls on camera. The footage was recorded from bus depot. Some of them have gotta go court. Hope they get lock up.

29th June 1998
Sleeping at Louise's again.

30th June 1998

Got home from Louise's at 7pm, mom was saying I take the piss and look at the time. She was saying that she gives me an inch and I take a mile. I cleaned the house and then just chilled out. Louise came here about 9:30pm, then we went back out. Moms performing again tonight. Janay's at a house and garage dance and Chana's sleeping at Sonia's. So, it's just been me and Louise here.

20th July 1998

Its Monday, its 11:37pm. I haven't written in here for ages, but here's the latest gossip. Elijah is out of prison; he did two months, now he's bangin' half of the town. THE TRAMP. I was screwin' when I heard but we aint really together, so I don't know why it bothered me. Not gonna lie, I've linked him a couple times myself. I know I shouldn't. It's so stupid. I must be fool.

Monique slept here last night.

27th July 1998

On Saturday I went to the best Shouters night ever. EVERYBODY was there.

1st August 1998

I looked out my window and saw a car that I didn't recognise. It wasn't someone from round here, I know who drives what round here. I thought it might be Elijah up to some kinda nonsense and trying to scare me. As I squeezed my eyes to see, it looked like there was a car seat in the passenger seat. My heart started to race. What's Elijah doing here with his daughters I thought?

I rushed down the stairs, quicker than a kid on Xmas Day. My teeth not brushed, pjs still on, bare foot like I live in those third world countries, I ran outside, but it wasn't Elijah's car.

I went over to Gaynor's and pushed the door handle like usual to see if it was one of the carers.

It wasn't'.

Eileen and Charlie had made it! They'd finally come down for the summer. Eileen told me she got my letter and said it pulled on her heart strings and that she couldn't believe such a young person like me could write such a heartfelt letter on behalf of her mom, she thanked me for taking the time to write the letter as it had encouraged her to make the trip to see Gaynor.

I asked how long she'd been down, she said she'd just come and that she'd been calling Gaynor, but she didn't want to wake her up as it was only 7:30am. I said nah let's go and wake her up, I knew how much she'd want to see Charlie. We crept up the stairs, we wanted to surprise her, not a peep.

We BURST open the bedroom door and shouted "SURPRISE!"

Gaynor didn't even flinch.

She was lying on her pastel green sheets, looking serene and peaceful, THUD.

My heart dropped out of my chest. I just knew it.

She was dead.

Eileen and Charlie were too late. My heart broke right there and then.

Eileen didn't even cry, I don't know if it was shock or guilt for not coming sooner. But she just froze. Charlie, didn't react, he probably thought his nan was sleeping. I doubt he even knew who she was, she was a stranger to him. I was shaking her frantically, begging her to wake up. But she never. When I turned around, Eileen and Charlie weren't there. I thought they must've gone downstairs. I stayed upstairs for what felt like ages, telling Gaynor to stop messing about and to wake up. Gaynor wasn't messing about though; the cancer had won.

FUK ME MAN-WHAT AM I GONNA DO?

I went downstairs to ask Eileen what we had to do, do we call the police, the hospital, or the doctors? Like, what's the process? Eileen wasn't downstairs, she must have gone for a walk to get some fresh air. When I rushed to the front door to see if her car was there, it wasn't. On the cabinet I noticed a note with my name on. It said' For Imani'.

I opened it, it said:
Imani, you are such a great girl, you've been like my mom's daughter when I haven't been there for her. I know how close you were to my mom and I feel that your grief is more worthy than mine. I let stubbornness, guilt and anger stop me from seeing my mom sooner and look, it's all been too late. For what. Even though I've not seen her for years, I wish I had made amends sooner. Your letter was the

reason I came down and that alone you should be proud of. I don't really know my mom; you know her more than me. I hope one day you'll be able to share some stories with me and Charlie, but for now, I can't stay here. This isn't my home and I feel like a hypocrite pretending to be that doting daughter that I haven't been. I'm not sure what to say really, but I'm sorry. I couldn't stand there pretending I was hurting the same way you were. I love my mom, and words can't explain how much I wish I could turn back the hands of time, from the whole incident with the money to me not coming to see her sooner. Too many things are runnin' on my mind, I've had to go. I hope you understand. This may be hard for you to understand because I know you're only young, but thanks for being there for my mom, I know she loved you like a daughter.

What a bitch. What a selfish bitch. She don't give a fuk, fuk you and fuk your letter. How could she get off like that, who just gets back in their fukin car? I'm writing this, and the tears are rolling down my face. I cannot believe she's gone. Whose gonna sort all this out, who am I gonna share stuff with now, whose gonna big me up when I pass my GCSE's, whose gonna be there when I get accepted to college or university?

Gaynor wake the fuk up and stop ramping.

I'm heartbroken. Not enough words can express the mixed feelings I have right now.

R I P Gaynor, you are loved.

time 2 grow up!

2nd August 1998

I've had enough. I genuinely have had enough. Gaynor's dead. This must be a dream. I'm gonna sort myself out and fix up for Gaynor. Fuk these boys who think they can treat me like an idiot, I'm gonna make sure I get myself together. I aint gonna link Elijah anymore either, I'm dun with it all man. I'm gonna get proper good grades and go to college and then to uni, no more fukin around after school. I know she'll look over me and have my back no atter what career I choose.

Gaynor, I'm doing this for you.

And just like that its summer 98, and this exercise book is nearly finished. I should have teefed a few more books from school 'cause now I aint got nothing to write in. But you know something, the amount of people that think its ok to read my diary. I might stop writing them. What's so interesting about my life that makes them wanna read MY business?

Imani Rochelle Evans signing out!
PEACE
LOVE
I CAN'T stand nosey people, you know the ones that go through people's personal business, reading all their shit, do you like nosey people?

A Word from the Author

Let me just take a moment to acknowledge; that little old me, Chantel, is actually writing the acknowledgement section of my very own book. That's quite a big deal and I'm truly proud (if I do say so myself!)

I do believe in faith and prayer and I asked God to help me live a life full of purpose and passion that aligned with my vision, I believe this book was an answer to that prayer. I dedicate time each day to reflect, meditate/pray and it's only right to acknowledge this and say thank you to Him for allowing this book to materialise.

This book has been in the making for quite some time and I'm grateful that I've been encouraged and inspired by others to complete it. I know its cliché, but I really did spend hours upon hours rewording and redrafting this book, but I've absolutely loved every minute of it. The crazy long hours that I put in flew by, I guess that's because I was doing something I truly became emersed in. So, the second acknowledgement is to me!! For the dedication, persistence, and drive to accomplish a lifelong goal. It all starts with believing in yourself.

Growing up in the 90s has clearly influenced some of the scenarios, and situations that Imani finds herself in. This book would not be possible if it weren't for the social observations I made whilst growing up in the West Midlands (Wolverhampton).

I grew up in an area where tower blocks and precincts played home to a host of criminal activities and where some members of the community struggled hugely with their mental Health (I didn't know that at the time). The area I grew up in was known for a prolific machete attack in 1996, the story gained huge media interest. So, events such as these have shaped some of the themes within the book, so I guess this is an acknowledgment to my hometown Wolverhampton; where we grew up quickly, learnt to become resilient and how to overcome challenges that life threw our way. Putting Wolverhampton on the map!

Now onto the tricky part of having to thank everyone who has supported this journey. Where do I even start? Well, even though the book has been in the making for several years, I guess the catalyst for the action was down to two books I read during the Covid-19 pandemic in 2020. The first book, Miracle Morning by Hal Elrod and the second, The Subtle Art of not giving a fuk by Mark Manson (both highly recommended). What these two books did for me was life changing. Sounds extreme I know, but both books helped me to realign my focus, re-evaluate my purpose and my values, and to really consider how I'd like to be remembered. With the entire world coming to a standstill during the pandemic, I knew it was time to write my book and get creative.

I recall telling my mom that I wanted to write a book and as expected she was incredibly supportive; it was my mom who recommended I use Marcia M Publishing House. My mom knows how busy I can be and how hard I work (normally to my own detriment!) And also reminds me to slow down and to make sure I rest too! Any fellow Capricorns will know how hard that can be for us, but we try! Either way, I just want to say thanks for the encouragement. Thanks mom. I also have to shout out my Dad, my brother Jamie, and my sister Charmadean for our childhood memories that have shaped who I have become, thanks.

A few weeks into the pandemic, I recall meeting up with my cousin and as usual we talked about personal development & business. I was about to share with him my excitement in starting my book, but just before I had chance to tell him, he said "Chantel, I think you should write a book." I nearly keeled over with excitement to announce that I had in fact started to write one, he's the very first person to see my story board, character profiles and my initial ideas on paper. One short paragraph doesn't do justice on how encouraging and supportive he is, and im profoundly grateful, thanks Richard Grizzle. Thanks to all my extended family who have also shown their support throughout this journey, much love to you all.

There's absolutely no way I can write a book and not give credit to two of my most inspirational teachers. My primary school teacher Mrs Favis, she read to the class every single day. I remember at the end of each school day a few minutes before the school bell, I would sit on the carpet and eagerly wait for her to read a few pages of a good book. I loved those carpet sessions. Listening to stories being read aloud was one of the most valuable and pleasurable experiences I recall having at Primary school. Story time exposed me to a rich variety of literature. This was followed by supportive and engaging discussions, where I was able to extend my world view and develop important critical thinking skills. My earliest memory was reading Crash Bang Wallop by Allan Ahlberg, and although I can't remember the plot, I'm almost sure my fond memories of the book stem from Mrs Favis's knack for great story telling.

The second teacher who really aided and shaped my writing skills was Mrs Newby. I loved English lessons at Secondary school and Mrs Newby really unearthed this passion from me. I recall one project where we had to compare the way in which both a Tabloid and Broadsheet newspaper covered the Death of Princess Diana; this is where I feel my writing skills were truly developed. Mrs Newby really encouraged me to give more and to do more on this project, she insisted I put

150% into this task and really routed for me, the hard work paid off; and I achieved top marks. Both teachers simultaneously evoked a passion within me for the love of English and I'm grateful for them both. Thank you.

*I have far too many friends to mention who have supported me with this book (and to be quite frank, if I even leave one of them out I'd never forgive myself) so, I'm going to thank you **ALL** from the bottom of my heart for your endless support. But special mentions are due to Chevonne Grappy, Zweana Bennett, Dionne Barrett, Kanika Fulcott, Barbara Russell, Marie Brown, Claudette Wynter, Carol Reid, Amanda Robinson, Zara Cleary, Amy Worrallo, Tamaan Wilkinson and Donna Dixon from supporting my initial idea, to supporting with blurb suggestions and providing me with feedback on my public speaking challenges!. I hope you've all enjoyed the book and now you've all got a little piece of me forever! Thank you ladies xx*

Tasiah Johnson, my daughter well... You saw first-hand the hours that rolled into days, that turned into nights and into extremely long shifts when working on the book. The nights I'd be typing till 4am and then get back up at 6am to continue, you saw the graft first-hand and saw how passionate I became. Thank you for encouraging me to rest and to take time out!. Thanks for the ideas you gave me, especially with the character Nina. Your ideas regarding her dress sense really helped capture Imani's hatred towards her (I knew your degree in Fashion Image Making and Styling would benefit me somehow!!) You know I'm all about doing things that you enjoy and living with passion and purpose and following your dreams, so if this book has taught you anything Tasiah, hopefully it's to live unreservedly and unapologetically yourself.

A special thank you to my partner who has supported me with various aspects of the book. Thanks for listening to my ideas (over and over and over again!!!) and sitting up with me until the early mornings on numerous occasions. He doesn't miss a trick when it comes to detail and design so who better than him to critique my work, he's honest and witty which made it all fun along the way, thanks.

Where would I be without my editor, Aisha. You made the editorial process so seamless, thank you so much for reading the book meticulously and editing it whilst keeping the authenticity that I wanted to capture. You really helped bring the book alive. Thank you.

From the start of the project, I knew the style I wanted to capture with the design of my first book. During my first consultation with Charlene Hemans, I knew she was the right person to design the cover and capture the essence of the 90's. You have done an amazing job on the cover and its everything I could have hoped for and more. Thank you so much.

Last but by no means least Marcia M, from Marcia Publishing house. The lady dubbed the 'Authors Midwife' and quite rightly so, because just like a midwife you were there to provide support during the entire process. Like a midwife who has roles and responsibilities that typically include pre and post antenatal care, you provided advice, ideas, hints and tips, character development suggestions, strategy meetings and a plethora of content through the MM Academy for writers. From our first telephone consultation you immediately showed huge interest in the idea and I knew I wanted to work alongside you. You saw something in the idea, and I recall coming off that call feeling extremely fired up and ready to send you my first 1000 word manuscript sample. I honestly cannot say thank you enough for being my 'midwife' along this process. Thank you so much.

And finally, a huge thank you to YOU. If you've made it this far, you certainly deserve a shout out! But I also hope that you enjoyed the book too!!

Thanks for taking time out to read and share my book, it's written from the heart and it means a lot that you've chosen to read it. There was no other motivating force when I decided to write this, except my love of the 90s and my love of writing, so I appreciate each and every purchase, thank you. There's something just for you on the next page...

BONUS CONTENT

An excerpt from 'Nina Unchained', the highly anticipated
second novel by Chantel Hall-Reid.

It was a cold, bleak, and foggy morning in the middle of December.

Winter was Nina's least favourite time of year. Having to get out of bed when it was still pitch dark was something she found particularly distressful. She hated having to "bundle up" in oversized jumpers in order to leave the house. And on top of that, trying to wrestle a toddler into a snowsuit, and then having to pick up his hat and gloves from out of the slush every five minutes was something she would rather not contend with, especially when she was in a rush, which was on most days.

She despised other car drivers being too scared to drive anywhere and often wondered whether it would be better to just walk, at least then she wouldn't feel like she was risking her life every time she got behind the wheel to go to work.

Recently Nina had been working her fingers to the bone, her working day usually started at 9am, but today she'd been requested to start at 6am. The traffic into work wasn't too bad, but there was a road closure. Nina thought about using her A-Z map but decided to rely on her own in-navigation system. She recently read somewhere that when humans use maps, they remember less about the places they go and put less work into generating their own internal picture. Nina had lived in Springten Green long enough to generate her own mental map of the area. She figured if she couldn't navigate herself down a street without having to get her A-Z out how would she ever navigate the much more complicated terrain of her life. So, she decided to get herself into work only using her own built-in navigational abilities.

The team needed to get a head start on a piece of copy for tomorrows editorial run and Nina didn't want to fail in supporting the team. Reece was still in his PJ's when she dropped him to Michelle, the childminder. She often felt guilty about dropping Reece off so early, but Marvin hadn't come home again, and Nina didn't have the time or energy to figure out where he may have laid his head to rest last night. Michelle was great, it wasn't the first time that Nina had text her in an emergency to have Reece because of Marvin's late-night escapades. Right now, Nina couldn't afford to lose her job, so Marvin's shenanigans would have to wait.

The Walker abduction story was gaining international coverage and was gripping millions from across the world, this was Nina's final chance to prove she could project manage such a high profile story. It'd been two years since she'd been given such a high profile case and back then Nina failed miserably. Sales that month were at the companies all time lowest, it came as a double blow when Surinder Patel from The Daily News also won the award for the best Journalist of the Year in the same month.

That morning was cold and bleak in the office, similar to today's weather. Sue was on the phone and the only part Nina heard was 'I promise I'll get it sorted; she's coming in the room now'. Sue turned to Nina and explained that it was Chief Executive Mrs Wright on the phone. Nina had only ever heard horror stories about Mrs Wright, so she already expected the worst. Sue informed Nina that due to the decrease in sales on the last story the company was now running at a financial loss and jobs were at stake. Mrs Wright wanted Nina fired. Tears started to roll down Nina's face, she needed this job. It was her first job since graduating and with Reece just 6 months old at the time, she certainly needed the money. Sue saw the pain in Nina's eyes and also knew how hard things had been for Nina recently with Reece and on-off boyfriend Marvin. Fortunately, Sue fought for Nina to stay, providing she undertook more training and CPD. That was Nina's first ever 'letter of concern'.

Nina was feeling relieved, just another hour before work was finished and she could collect Reece from Michelle. It had been an extremely long day and she was looking forward to spending some much needed time with him. She sipped on more black coffee in a bid for the next hour to pass by more quickly. Working in Journalism meant that deadlines and long working days were common, but Fridays were great because it was definitely a 4.30pm finish. Whilst Nina didn't always agree with Sue's management style, she did agree with her commitment to ensuring staff had an early finish on a Friday. Nina hadn't seen Sue at all today, there'd been another plot twist in the abduction story, so everyone figured Sue was up to her eyes with work and was just stuck in her office.

"Nina, Nina Harington-Bechtel, I know it's getting late, but I've looked at the copy you've submitted on the abduction of Emily Walker, it's not quite hitting the right notes for me, it needs more pizazz and definitely hasn't been fact checked correctly. This is the biggest story of the year; it needs to sell. Our sales targets weren't met last month, this is your last chance before the year comes to an end to ensure we surpass The Daily News's sales. I won't have them beat us again this month Nina. We need this going out on the print run tomorrow morning."

Nina looked up from her desk where she had begun to slouch to determine who was screeching in the high-pitched tone. She didn't recognise the lady who was stood in front of her.

She had a curious eclectic style about her. She was dressed head to toe in jet black. Around her throat there was a leopard-patterned scarf and wound around her head a turban of the same material. Her skin was awfully pale, and she was wearing bright red glasses. Her waist was small, in fact anorexic-looking. The woman didn't even look past 30. She had long, black-dyed hair - pierced eyelid - tattoo of a sword on her wrist; probably several more under her black attire. This wasn't punk fashion. This was someone saying, stay the fuck away from me, mixed with class and trepidation. What an unusual style thought Nina.

Before Nina could get a word in; the woman turned the piece of paper back to her and added sternly,
"When can you get it corrected?"

Nina didn't quite know what to do or say, she'd been working on the copy since 6am and Sue had always been supportive of the copy's Nina submitted. Besides, who was this lady? Nina knew it would take at least another 3-4 hours to re-edit the copy. Nina couldn't face the humiliation of texting Michelle begging for an extension AGAIN. Worse still that the fees for late pickups had recently been increased. The last invoice for childcare fees were the highest they'd ever been. Nina often wondered if the hours she worked were worth it, especially when she could barely make ends meet.
Nina hesitated and mumbled,

"It's going to take over three hours and I need to get my son from the childminders, Sue says on Fridays we can leave at 4.30pm." She spoke so quietly she wasn't even sure her voice had been heard.

"You don't work for Sue anymore Nina, I'm Chief Executive Debbie Miranda Wright, but you'll call me Mrs Wright. I'll be the one you answer to from now on. The world of journalism requires flexibility. Your job is to polish and refine a story and what I've just received isn't fit for publication. YOU ARE responsible for fact checking and the whole things a mess. It's no wonder we've had to fire Sue; accepting that type of submission, that kind of copy is embarrassing for us here at The Morning News. I'll leave it with you and trust that you'll have the documents ready before you leave today. I've told the security staff and the cleaners that they'll be here all night, so if they can stay, so can you," proclaimed Mrs Wright.

"But…" Nina tried to reply, it was too late, Mrs Wright had already spun round on her slate black Alexander McQueen heels and was out of the door before Nina could finish her sentence.

MARCIA M
PUBLISHING HOUSE

www.marciampublishing.com